Feeling her pet
arms pushed all
age differe

Thoughts of how right she felt underneath him when they were making out on the bed of leaves, how he'd come so close to making love to her and how her mouth tasted like the sweetest candy he had ever savored pushed past any common sense he had. The only thing he could think of was to finish what they had started earlier.

He allowed his lips to plunder and peruse. She opened to him automatically and her tongue met his with matching passion and desire. As he suckled on her soft lips, he couldn't help but roam her body. Her delicate curves had his mind spinning. Before he knew it, he had picked her up and carried her into the nearest bedroom. As he fell back on the bed, he pulled her on top of him and continued to caress her lips with his own.

He would never get tired of kissing her. Her groans hinted that she might feel a fraction of the same thing he was feeling....

He wanted her. He had to have her.

Now.

Books by Gwyneth Bolton

Kimani Romance

If Only You Knew
Protect and Serve
Make It Hot
The Law of Desire

GWYNETH BOLTON

became an avid romance fan after sneak-reading her mother's romance novels. In the nineties, she was introduced to African-American romance novels and her life hasn't been the same since. She has a B.A. and an M.A. in creative writing and a Ph.D. in English. She teaches writing and women's studies at the college level. When she is not writing African-American romance novels, she is curled up with a cup of herbal tea, a warm quilt and a good book. She currently lives in Syracuse, New York, with her husband, Cedric. Readers can contact her via e-mail at gwynethbolton@prodigy.net or visit her Web site at www.gwynethbolton.com.

THE LAW

OF DESIRE

Gwyneth Bolton

HIGHTOWER HONORS
FOUR BROTHERS ON A MISSION TO PROTECT, SERVE AND LOVE...

KIMANI™
ROMANCE

To my sands…

Kimmie, Shakira, Antoinette, Edith, Audrey, Monica, Sherita and Karen.

I will always cherish our sisterhood
and the bond we share.

Yours in Delta…

KIMANI PRESS™

ISBN-13: 978-0-373-86094-4
ISBN-10:   0-373-86094-3

Recycling programs
for this product may
not exist in your area.

THE LAW OF DESIRE

www.kimanipress.com

Printed in U.S.A.

Dear Reader,

The woman Lawrence Hightower finds himself extremely attracted to could be a criminal, and he makes it his business to find out the real deal, by any means necessary. He is a by-the-book, highly decorated police detective. The last thing he needs is an attraction to a little thug of a girl with more attitude than should be legal!

Minerva Jones needs to keep a low profile until she is sure the person who killed her brother doesn't come for her next. Having a cop check her out, even in a hey-baby-you're-*fine* kind of way, is not something she needs. But things happen…and sometimes what you think you *don't* need is exactly the thing that will set you free. Lawrence is a good guy with a bit of an edge or a bad boy who's well-meaning and good-natured, depending on what day you catch him. Minerva is an innocent pretending to be a ride-or-die chick. They are so *right* for one another it feels *wrong*. Neither of them are what they seem. No wonder they set off each other's radars from the moment they meet! Their journey to love is full of passion, drama, a little intrigue and undeniable heat.

I'm so glad you've decided to take the ride with Lawrence and Minerva. Please be on the lookout for the final installment of the Hightower series, *Sizzling Seduction*. Patrick Hightower has been dodging love long enough, and something tells me he will go down fast and hard. *Sizzling Seduction* is slated for release in October 2009.

Gwyneth Bolton

Acknowledgments

First I want to thank God for the many blessings in my life, especially the blessing to share my stories. I'd like to thank my family: my mother, Donna, my sisters Jennifer, Cassandra, Michelle and Tashina, my nieces Ashlee and Zaria and my husband, Cedric. And I'd like to thank all the readers who have taken the time to write me and let me know what they thought of my novels. Your words have meant more than you could ever know.

Prologue

"Surprise!" The gleeful voices greeted her as soon as she opened the door.

M. Athena Jones—the "M" stood for Minerva, a name she hadn't willingly gone by since her mom died—clutched her chest as she entered the two-bedroom apartment she used to share with her brother.

It was still a full two weeks before the summer semester was over but she had turned in her last paper and had officially finished her undergraduate degree. As exciting as it was, she certainly wasn't expecting a surprise party.

"I had to do something special. And I had to make sure your smart behind wouldn't figure it out." Her brother, Calvin, picked her up and spun her around. "Did it work?"

Calvin placed her carefully back on the floor and she gazed up at him. He'd taken after their father in the height department and towered over her petite frame by at least a foot. His caramel complexion and the deep waves of his recently cut Caesar made for a dapper combination. He was wearing his usual khakis and Chucks. His handsome face even gleamed with a rare smile.

"Yes! Oh, my God, Calvin. You didn't have to do this. I thought we were going to do our usual." Her eyes welled up as she looked at the streamers and balloons that decorated the apartment.

"Oh, we're still going to have our usual celebration. You know we have to keep up tradition. But this is special, baby girl. It's not every day that my little sister gets her degree! I'm proud of you, girl." Calvin hugged her again.

In two weeks she would walk the stage and receive her bachelor's degree from California State University-Northridge. At twenty-six years old, she had finally managed to work her way through school and get her degree. Two classes here and one class there…it had added up. She had had to work her way through school because her family didn't have a lot of money when she'd graduated from high school. So she went right into the workforce, taking jobs that she'd hated, but always keeping her eyes on the prize.

One degree down and one to go.

She hoped to have her master's of social work degree by the time she was thirty—thirty-five the latest.

A girl could dream...

Her voice caught as she greeted everyone. She had almost called her brother to let him know that she couldn't stop by. But if she had stayed in her own small apartment to fill out grad school applications, she would have missed this.

There weren't that many people there, only a few in fact. But everyone there held special meaning to the two of them. They'd lost their parents when they were young and even before that her older brother was the one who really raised her.

Valerie Monroe, the social worker who worked with them so that she could remain with her brother after their mother died, was there along with Taj and Pam, two of her closest friends from childhood, and a few other folks from the neighborhood.

She couldn't believe that because of her quest to finish her degree and "make it" she could scarcely remember the last time she'd seen them. She still called Valerie every couple of weeks just to check in. But she had lost contact with Taj and Pam completely. None of her friends from work or school were there. She didn't have many at either place. With school and work she didn't have a lot of time for socializing.

Friends from work and school wouldn't have fit in at the party, anyway. She remembered reading W. E. B. DuBois's book *The Souls of Black Folk* in one of her Africana studies classes and mused that she needed more than the concept of double consciousness to describe the fractured feeling in her life. More like triple consciousness. Sometimes it felt as if she had one face for her work life as office manager in a predominantly white law firm, one face as a college student, and one for her friends in the neighborhood and her brother. One day she would find a way to make all her worlds fit together.

Normally, she and Calvin celebrated all milestones with a night out for dinner. Her brother would let her pick the restaurant and tell her that she could pick the most expensive place in town. She always picked Roscoe's House of Chicken 'n Waffles. They ate there when she completed middle school, high school, and when she got her job as an office clerk at Henderson, Moore & Moore, the law firm where she still worked.

The banner on the wall read CONGRATULATIONS THENA! That was big for her brother. He was the last remaining holdout when it came to her name. She'd pretty much decided after her mother died that she would go by Thena, the shortened version of her middle name. He had pretty much decided that the name their mother named her Minerva, was just fine.

Minerva Athena Jones didn't know what had possessed her mother to name her after not one but two goddesses of wisdom. She *did* know that neither name made her the coolest girl in class growing up. The only thing she hated more than people calling her Minerva was when they called her Minnie. It made her skin crawl. So until she could officially change her name she went by M. Athena Jones. Friends called her Thena.

She took off the cream linen jacket that went with

the matching pencil skirt she was wearing. Like most of her clothing, she'd gotten the smart and sassy business suit on sale.

She hugged and greeted the rest of the guests and kept looking back to smile at Calvin. Who knew he was so sentimental? She knew he loved her without a doubt. He was just a guy's guy and didn't always express his feelings outwardly.

"So what are you going to do now that you're done with school?" Valerie was leaning against the wall in the kitchen. She and Thena both watched Calvin taking some heat while he took chicken wings out of the oven.

"My baby sis is going to get more education. She's just like our mother. She's smart and she's going to live the life Mama should've lived." Calvin answered Valerie's question before Thena could.

Thena smiled and let her brother bask in his happiness. He'd practically raised her when their mother died. He had just turned eighteen at the time, and she'd been twelve. Things were hard. But they had made it and they'd been able to stay together until she moved out on her own three years ago. He deserved to be proud. It was because of his tough love and firm hand that she was able to do much of what she had done.

If only their mother could see Thena now. She'd sing for joy.

Their mother had a voice that would have put the Queen of Soul to shame. She had come to California from Alabama with stars in her eyes. All hopes of stardom got put on hold, though, when she'd met and soon married a guitarist and gave birth to a son. Six years later she'd given birth to a baby girl and soon after that her husband's recreational drug use spiraled out of control, making him take risks not only with his own life but with hers, as well. Neither of them made it.

It was Calvin who'd encouraged Thena to further her education. He kept books around for her to read from the time she first learned how. He made sure she did all her homework over the years.

Sure, Calvin was strict and might have been the reason at least two of Thena's former boyfriends ended up in the hospital badly beaten, but underneath his brash persona lay the man who stayed up all night with her whenever she'd been sick. *Complicated* didn't even begin to describe Calvin, or Thena's feelings for him.

"I hope to get my MSW eventually and go into social work like you, Val. You've inspired me so much."

"You'll be a great at it." Valerie offered with a smile as she helped Calvin place the wings on the plastic serving tray.

When Calvin went to answer the door, Thena and Valerie worked together to ready the rest of the food. They carried the platters out to Calvin's living room, which was filled with royal-blue crushed velvet furniture.

"Yeah, sorry man. I thought I told you about the party. Must have thought I did when I actually hadn't." Calvin walked toward the living room with his best friend David Sims following him.

Thena'd been wondering where David was and just assumed that he was off wheeling and dealing somewhere. He was a serial entrepreneur at Langer and Associates, launching, developing and making small businesses profitable. And he was one of Calvin's *only* noncriminal, non-gang-banging friends. David and Calvin had grown up together on the South Central streets, but David had gone the school and college route. She looked up to David almost as much as she looked up to her brother.

She ran over and gave David a hug.

"Hey, baby girl. Sorry I almost missed the celebration. Calvin neglected to tell me about it. Good thing I was in the neighborhood and decided to stop by." David hugged her close before letting her go.

"It's okay. I'm glad you made it and I hope you can stay. I know you're busy."

"Never too busy for you—" David started.

"Hey, sis, get in here and blow out the candles on this cake. I got your favorite, with pineapple filling." Calvin interrupted David by pulling her away and leading her to the cake.

She frowned and shook her head. Her brother could be so controlling at times. She cast an apologetic glance at David and he just shrugged nonchalantly and winked at her.

She figured if David wasn't irritated with her brother, then she shouldn't be, either. When two men were friends as long as they'd been friends, they probably had disagreements and bounced back from them more than times she could count. And that sheet cake with the pineapple filling was calling her name.

After everyone left, Calvin gave her a ride back to her apartment. And she was glad to have the one-on-one time with her brother. Seeing everyone meant a lot to her. She had let too many relationships fall to the wayside, and she needed to reconnect. It was a good thing it wasn't too late to do so. And as soon as she finished her grad school applications she was going to start working on rebuilding her friendships and her relationship with her brother. *Girl from the 'hood makes good.*

"Thanks, Calvin. That celebration was so special."

"You know I had to do something special for this, baby girl. You made it. Mama would be so proud." He smiled and kept his eyes on the road, as 50 Cent's "Many Men" started playing. Calvin reached over to turn it up while bouncing his head to the grim lyrics.

"Do you really think Mama would be proud?"

"Hell, yeah… She made me promise her before she passed that I would make sure you got your education and didn't get caught up with no boys. She wanted to be sure you at least got your high school diploma. Trust me, she'd be proud. You're all upwardly mobile now! You even dress all fancy."

"Well…since I've clearly exceeded her wishes now…" She flipped from his CD changer to the radio and changed 50 Cent to Maroon Five.

Now that's more like it! A nice happy tune about love on "Sunday Morning," not maudlin lyrics about men wishing death on someone… What is it with gang bangers, rappers and death wishes anyway?

"Do you think you can ease up and stop scaring away my boyfriends?"

"First, *Minerva,* never touch a black man's radio." He turned the CD changer back and restarted the 50 Cent song from the beginning. "And second, boyfriends? You got some boyfriends I haven't scared away yet? Who are they? What're their names?"

She punched him on the arm, not enough to hurt him but enough to sting, she hoped. "Come on, Calvin. It's not funny. I'd like to get married and have kids one day. That won't happen if you don't stop blocking!"

She couldn't help feeling a little irritated. When she was in high school, two of the boys she had started dating ended up getting jumped and beaten severely. Calvin always said he hadn't had anything to do with it. But after the second one, her conscience wouldn't allow her to date a guy knowing he might get hurt because of her, not to mention that having a crazy gang-banging brother scared a lot of guys away.

"What do you know about blocking?" Calvin teased as he eased the car onto her block.

"Stop laughing. It's not funny. I'm twenty-six years old. I think it's time I started living my life."

"You need protecting. Look at what happened to Mama." Calvin's voice took on that serious, brother-knows-best tone. "This world is rough. You wouldn't survive without me to protect you. I couldn't protect Mama because I was just a kid. But I'll protect you with my life, Minerva. And that's real talk. Trust me, when the right guy comes around, I'll know and I'll let *you* know. For now, just focus on getting those degrees and making your big brother proud."

She let out an exasperated breath and rolled her eyes. There was no talking to Calvin and certainly no way to get him to see how stifling he was being. In fact, he saw that as his main purpose in life since their mom had passed away. Sometimes she wished she didn't have a big brother.

"So I'll see you in a few days for dinner at our spot, right?" He pulled up to her apartment building.

"Yes, Calvin, I'll be there." She got out and walked inside.

Where is he?

She glanced at her watch. It was telling her she might have been stood up. Usually when her brother said he would meet her somewhere, he got there before she did. Of the two of them, she was the chronically late one. And today she was running late from work. That's why when she got to Roscoe's House of Chicken 'n Waffles and found that she had beaten him there she should have known something was wrong.

After waiting an hour with no sign of Calvin, she decided he must have made good on his threat to leave the next time she kept him waiting. She finished her meal alone and ordered one special to go before getting on the bus heading toward her brother's apartment.

Standing and brushing the crumbs off her navy-blue-and-white pin-striped suit with wide leg pants and a double-breasted jacket, she shook her head. Calvin was probably mad at her. But the meal would be her peace offering. Although she didn't know why he wasn't used to her perpetual lateness by now. He didn't have to pick tonight to set an example and leave. It was their official graduation celebration, after all.

But his door was open when she got to his apartment.

That wasn't a good sign.

Given some of Calvin's unsavory business dealings, a busted open door signaled either a police raid or a rival gang's hit. She never thought the day would come when she would be hoping for the former.

Feeling like the stereotypical hapless and clueless teen beauty in a horror flick, she pushed open the door and went in.

Things were strewn all over the normally neat living room. Papers covered the floor and Calvin's coveted Crip-blue crushed-velvet sofa had been turned upside down, the pillows torn to pieces. She didn't have to walk too far into the room to see her brother.

He lay on the floor with a bullet in the middle of his forehead.

Thena's legs threatened to give way and she stumbled, dropping the container of food. Somehow she managed not to hit the floor along with the fluffy waffles and crispy chicken.

Her handsome, tall, strong and protective older brother, the only constant in her life, lay dead. Her heart dropped and her knees buckled. She hit the floor with a thud and her hand flew to her mouth. She wanted to scream but no sound came out. The air was as empty as she felt.

How could this be happening?

She reached out and touched his caramel face. His eyes were still open and she moved her hand over them to shut the lids.

Her heart felt as if it had exploded in her chest the pain was so deep. Tears fell, feeling hot and scorching against her skin. She grabbed her chest and gasped before she realized she wasn't alone.

Someone was in the back room throwing things around, obviously looking for something. Whoever it was must have heard her because the shuffling stopped.

Somehow, even with the ever-expanding hole in her heart, the pronounced lack of air and the absence of any rational thought, she was able to pull herself up from her brother's side and run. She dashed out of the apartment building and ran as if her life depended on it.

The burning tears cooled somewhat with her sprint, but they kept falling. She ran for blocks and blocks before she had to stop. The vision of her brother with a hole in his head stuck in her mind until the food she'd eaten at Roscoe's would no longer sit in her stomach. Everything came barreling back up and out, projecting forward and hitting the cement before she could even come to a full stop. She fell to her knees and sobbed as she vomited. The navy-blue headband that held back her shoulder-length natural curls popped off her head and landed in the mess.

She had never felt so empty in all her life.

Realizing that whoever was in the apartment hadn't followed her, she didn't know what to do. She thought about going back to his place and calling the cops, but decided to go home and get cleaned up first. She could call the cops once she got rid of the tears and the sour taste in her mouth.

The emptiness, the guilt, the loss, all threatened to consume her, to eat her alive. What was she supposed to do without Calvin?

When she got home she saw, David Sims sitting in front of her building in his luxury car waiting for her. The tall, golden, honey-complexioned man stepped out of his car and walked up to her. She couldn't think of anyone better to be waiting for her at this time.

"David." She ran right into his arms. "Oh, my God, David…Calvin is…Calvin…I just came from his house and…" She took a deep breath. She couldn't say it. She couldn't say the words; her brother was dead.

"I know. It's bad. He was into some serious stuff this time. I tried to bail him out, but I got there too late." He took a short step away, placed his hand under her chin and tilted her head so that he was looking right into her eyes. "Did you see anything?"

She gazed up at him. "There was someone there looking for something when I walked in. I heard noises in the back of the apartment and I ran. I ran and I haven't even called the police yet. I have to call the police and—"

"I must have gotten there after you. Because there was no one there when I got there. I did make an anonymous call from a phone booth to the police." He shook his head. "The thing is, baby girl, according to your brother, the people he got on the wrong side of are *not* the kind of people you want thinking you know anything or saw something. And they have folks in the LAPD on their payroll. If they thought you knew anything they would have no problem killing you, too." The warning in his voice and the stern expression on his face made her heart stop.

"I didn't see anyone. I don't know anything."

"You can tell me if you do. Did Calvin give you anything recently? Did he tell you anything?"

Besides the surprise party, he hadn't given her anything. And besides his typical warnings—about staying away from guys and making sure to run anyone interested in her past him because too many people might see her as an easy mark to get back at him—he hadn't told her anything.

"No, he didn't and I don't know anything."

"Okay. We still can't risk the cops questioning you and those folks thinking you might know something. Some of the things Calvin told me about them…" He shook his head. "Trust me, you don't want to mess with them. You have to get out of L.A. It wouldn't be good for them to find out you spoke to the cops, especially if they saw you leaving Calvin's place." David rubbed his chin, while keeping a careful eye on her.

She tried to hold it together, because she didn't want to appear like some weak-willed woman who couldn't deal. She gulped in an attempt to swallow the fast-growing lump in her throat.

"I can't just up and leave. I don't have anywhere to go. And what about Calvin? I have to bury my brother! I can't just leave."

"You don't have a choice." His face went hard and serious before he softened slightly. "You were the most important person in the world to Calvin. The only family he had. He wouldn't even let a straight-laced guy like me try and kick it to you because he felt I wasn't good enough for you." David gave a rueful smile at the memory. "And I was his best friend. So I feel obligated to look out for you and make sure the cops don't unwittingly put you in danger. I have some folks in Jersey you could stay with until the danger passes. You remember my twin cousins, Timmy and Tommy McKnight?"

She remembered the twins who used to hang out with Calvin and David before moving back East. They had been members of the same gang as her brother. She nodded.

"Well, they're probably the only people besides me that would feel strongly about protecting Calvin's little sister." He ran his thumb across her cheek, wiping away endless tears.

She willed herself to be stronger. "Why would they feel obligated? I doubt they even remember me."

"Because Calvin, Timmy and Tommy all started banging around the same time. They share a bond." He glanced down the street, no longer looking her in the eye, as he finished. "And even though I never went there with them, I know how seriously they took their affiliation."

"Are they still banging?"

"I have no idea. I doubt it." He turned and glanced at her briefly. "We need to get you out of here before the cops start questioning you. Come on."

"But don't I need to pack or—"

"No. You don't have time. I'll give you enough cash to get some things when you get there. We need to leave here now." He glanced away again. "I also have something for you to give to my cousins. It's just a jacket…a family heirloom of sorts… It used to belong to my dad…their uncle. But I need you to give me the keys to your place and Calvin's."

She bit back a sob. This couldn't be happening. This was supposed to be the happiest time in her life. She was going to finally get that nice pretty diploma to hang on her wall. She was going to show her brother that all the sacrifices he had made for her and everything he'd done to raise her when their parents died was worth it. And now he was dead and she had to go on the run.

"When the coast is clear, I'll be able to send you your things and get into his place and see if they left anything you might want. I'm so sorry this happened, baby girl. But I'm going to help you. Because I know Calvin would've wanted me to help you. And don't worry. I'll be coming for you when it's safe."

He opened up his car door as he spoke and guided her in.

She took one last look at her apartment complex as she got in the vehicle. She had no idea how her life could have taken such a drastic turn in a matter of hours, but she did know things would never be the same again. She just felt lucky to have Calvin's best friend looking out for her. And she hoped Timmy and Tommy McKnight had her back the way their cousin David did. *My life depends on it.*

Chapter 1

One month later...

"Now, you're looking like a *real* down-ass chick."
Timmy McKnight reached out and touched the bright
auburn extensions that had been placed in Minerva's—
no more M. Athena for a woman on the run—hair at
the Dominican beauty salon.

The beautician at Esmerelda's Beauty Salon had
glued the auburn weave tracks in layered spots of
Minerva's dark-brown hair. The extensions mixed in
and gave her a two-toned look without her having to
dye it. And the amount of spray, mousse and gel piled
on her hair made her normally soft curls hard and card-
board straight. She looked like a mix between Cruella

De Vil remixed with Remy Ma and lots of auburn hair color.

I hate it.

Between the outlandish hairstyle and the Baby Phat outfit she had purchased in downtown Paterson, she felt like a different person. Just a little over a month ago she wouldn't have been caught dead looking like a hoochie mama. Now her life depended on being able to blend in and appear to be the type of girl who would actually hang out with Timmy and Tommy McKnight.

She had no choice.

She had spent the majority of the money David had given her to get lots of things she would have never worn before. Lots of Apple Bottom, Rocawear and other hip-hop brand names made up her wardrobe now. No more Michael by Michael Kors or Bitten by Sarah Jessica Parker—even if it was on sale—for a while.

David had been *really* generous when it came to giving her the funds she'd needed to relocate. She vowed to make it up to him one day. Her brother's life of crime had put David in the awkward position of having to lie to the police about her whereabouts and who knew what he had to promise his cousins to get them to help her.

"Yeah, you're looking real ride-or-die, baby girl. You can roll with us now," Tommy nodded in approval. As he moved his head, his shoulder-length dreadlocks bounced.

Hair was the one thing that allowed her to tell the two identical, mocha-complexioned twins apart. Timmy wore his hair low-cut with brush-waves. They were each the same medium height. Timmy was a little bulkier than Tommy in size.

As nice as they had been to her, Minerva didn't want to *roll* with them. She just wanted to stay home. But they didn't like the idea of leaving her alone just yet.

The three of them ended up at a nice bar downtown. It was packed and bustling with energy.

From what she could tell about the city of Paterson, it seemed like a fairly segregated place. The neighborhood where she lived with the McKnights was predominantly black and poor. She thought she'd seen ghettos growing up in South Central, but nothing could have prepared her for what she saw living on Governor Street in Paterson. There were always people out and about, but no one ever saw anything when something went down. The run-down tenements didn't seem habitable; but they were overflowing with tenants. Some of the dilapidated buildings made where she grew up in South Central look like the suburbs. At least they had trees and houses back in Cali.

Thena, now Minerva, needed the semi-makeover to be able to walk down the street and not get robbed or otherwise victimized. Her little "Cali office girl" style was not going cut it here so she had to adapt.

"Have you heard from David?" Tommy gave her a probing stare and interrupted her reverie about her 'hood status and staying alive in Paterson.

"Not in a couple of weeks," Minerva answered. "He said he'd slack off calling until things cooled down.

They still haven't figured out who killed my brother."
She felt her voice choke but she willed herself to keep
it together.

She had cried the entire bus trip from California to
New Jersey. But she refused to turn into a babbling
brook in front of Timmy and Tommy. She knew she had
to be tough, even though she was walking around with
this gaping hole in her chest. *More like in my heart.*

Putting on a brave face didn't stop her heart from
pounding. She understood that she had to be strong. But
how could she when the pain sometimes went so deep
that she felt she could barely breathe?

She had left without burying her brother.

And she could just see her parents and Calvin in
heaven looking down on her with disappointment. They
were supposed to always take care of one another. He'd
been the overprotective big brother and she did what
she could by learning to cook and take care of their day-
to-day living. He had always come through for her and
she had let him down when it really counted.

The guilt she felt threatened to overwhelm her. She
felt like it would suffocate her.

"Well, well, well…if it isn't Timothy and Thomas
McKnight. What are you two doing here? I hope
you're not scoping out the place as a spot for illegal
drug distribution."

Minerva looked up and into the most intense brown
eyes she'd ever seen. The man who had pulled up a
chair, straddled it backwards and interrupted their conversation had a perfectly chiseled face with bold and

strong features. In addition to the seriously penetrating stare, he had a five-o'clock shadow that gave him a rough and rugged appearance. His full lips didn't seem like they ever smiled, *ever*. But that didn't take away from the fact he was fine. Fine with a capital *F*.

Fine and he has cop written all over him. Minerva looked him up and down.

"Detective." Tommy nodded and focused on the drink in front of him.

"Wow…if it isn't my favorite narc, Detective Hightower. I would ask if you'd like to join us. But seeing as you already have… What can we do for you this fine evening?" Timmy, the older twin didn't seem like he was one to hold back.

The cop turned his direction toward her.

Great, was all she could think as the detective hit her with his x-ray-vision stare. The last thing she needed was for some cop to get her on his radar.

"And who're you?" Detective Hightower was looking at her so closely she wanted to bolt.

Damn, his deep voice is sexy.

Instead, she pursed her lips before rolling her eyes and letting out a deep, overly dramatic breath. "Who wants to know and why?"

His eyes narrowed slightly.

She narrowed her eyes right back at him. She never liked bullies and this "detective" had bullying down to an art form. He had some nerve just inviting himself to their table and grilling everyone as if he didn't need a reason.

And then there was the stir in the pit of her stomach that seem to kick up to a fevered pitch when he looked at her. It wasn't fear, no, that would have been too much like right. No, the things she felt just staring in his eyes and having him so close caused her to feel things like want and need.

"This is Minnie Samuels, Detective Hightower. She's a good friend visiting us from California." Tommy offered the information a little too freely for her taste. And apparently Timmy's, too, because his twin brother turned and glared at him at the same time she did.

The three of them had decided to just change her last name and have her go by her childhood nickname, Minnie—which she hated more than she did her actual name—in order to keep things simple. But they'd also decided that her "name" would only be divulged on a need-to-know basis. She and Timmy clearly had different ideas about who needed to know.

She gritted her teeth in irritation. The cop annoyed her and caused her heart to flutter at the same time, and she had just met the man. "I'll be back. I need to powder my nose."

She stood and went looking for the ladies' room without so much as a second glance back. She did take the liberty of cursing the smug cop out in her head as she walked away, imagining all the ways she could read him up, down and sideways if he was still there when she got back. While she had never developed the unhealthy, hateful and distrusting relationship to cops that her brother and others in her neighborhood had, she could see herself heading in that direction fairly quickly if she had to deal with Detective Hightower much longer.

She really hadn't had to use the rest room or fix her makeup. She wasn't even wearing that much makeup. Just a little foundation, eyeliner, mascara, lipstick and lip gloss. It was a lot more than she normally wore, though. Typically, she couldn't be bothered with more than a little lip gloss. But she figured a girl who wore hip-hop designer clothing like the hot-pink, skin-tight Baby Phat denim minidress she was sporting and rocking two-toned hair would have on foundation and lipstick at the *very* least. She drew the line at eye shadow and blush, though. And there was no way she would get any long fake acrylic nails. There was only so much she was willing to do for appearances.

She looked in the mirror, surveyed her outfit and cringed.

This *is so-oo not me...*

Hoping the cop was gone, she decided to head back out to their table and try to talk the McKnight twins into calling it an evening. The sooner she was out of the flashy clothes and into some sweats the better.

She walked out of the ladies' room and right into the nosy detective. He must have been standing in the narrow hallway waiting for her. He pretty much blocked the way back into the bar so she decided to lean against the wall and wait for him to be a gentleman and get out of her way. Heart thumping and pulse racing, she folded her arms across her chest and twisted her lips to the side.

A full minute must have passed with him just standing there staring at her like he was trying to figure out one of the great mysteries of the world. She huffed and moved to go around him. He grabbed her forearm and moved her back.

A tingle raced across her arm and landed smack-dab in her heart. At such close proximity, the masculine scent of him assaulted her nose and sparked a keening need in her gut. She took a deep, calming breath that she hoped looked like she had an attitude and not like she had been shaken to her core.

"Can I help you with anything, Detective? I couldn't imagine what. But you *must* have some reason for making yourself a nuisance this evening, especially since you don't know me and have no *reasonable* cause to harass me." She tilted her head to the side partly for appearance's sake but mostly because it helped with the sudden feeling of vertigo this man had her experiencing.

He looked puzzled for a moment before his lips formed a slight snarl. "You hanging with the McKnight twins is all the cause I need to keep an eye on you, Miss… Samuels."

"So the whole 'innocent until proven guilty' thing is just a cute idea for a fairy tale or are you really an officer of the *law?*" She folded her arms across her chest and swallowed. She had no idea what had come over her, but she knew she refused to back down and let some cop punk her.

"Oh, so you're a little smart-ass? You should ask your friend Timmy McKnight what happens to smart-asses in jail. 'Cause that's where you're headed if you keep moving in the wrong circles. I don't know you but I know plenty of dumb little girls like you who get caught up, carrying weight across state lines, holding things they shouldn't be holding in their purses…" He glanced at the small leather handbag she was carrying.

"Tell me something, what do you think I'd find if I took a look through that bag of yours? Maybe something you used to *powder your nose?* Would that be foundation or coke?" He leaned forward and she instinctively leaned forward, as well.

The nerve of this man! The amount of incredulity coursing through her only hinted at how shocking she found his entire demeanor.

They were standing so close to each other in the small hallway that it was impossible for her not to imagine his lips swooping down and covering hers. She licked her lips and swallowed. *What might that kiss be like, taste like, feel like.*

She noticed him swallowing too. *Is he imagining the same thing?*

She looked him up and down taking in every inch of his muscular physique. She'd never found herself so attracted to a man before. The lean, hard frame in front of her, wearing jeans, sneakers and a white T-shirt was just too sexy and too aggravating for words… And certainly too fine to be a cop…

Why was the first adult male to make her pulse

quicken and her heart race a member of the police force?

"Don't you have anything better to do than to harass people who aren't doing anything wrong? Or is that what cops are getting paid for these days?"

"You need to—"

"Hey, bro, we've been looking all over for you. You need to get back over there so we can finish celebrating. You know I'm going to be heading out to make it home to my wife and Joel can barely wait to get back to his new fiancée…" The voice of the man who interrupted them trailed off when he noticed her standing there. He was a younger version of the detective and she got a cop vibe from him, as well.

"You need some help here, bro?" The younger one gave her the once-over. He had that penetrating gaze thing down and she wondered if it was a cop thing or a family trait.

They were certainly related. She could tell because they both shared the same ruggedly handsome looks and tall, fine, muscular frames. If that wasn't enough, they had the same bold brown eyes. But the younger one had a light in his eyes that hinted at immense happiness whereas her detective…

My detective? Oh, brother… The annoying, mean and irritating detective had a hard, impenetrable glare in his eyes. She couldn't see any happiness there.

"I'm cool, Jason. I was just trying to warn Miss Samuels here about the company she keeps. But you know what they say…you can't save 'em if they don't want to be saved." He shrugged in a nonchalant manner. "So, I'll just leave you with this. Stay out of trouble or it will be my pleasure to show you what cops get paid for." He turned and walked away.

The younger one stared at her for a moment and shrugged. "I suggest you take heed and watch the company you keep. We're not soft on crime around here. And the fact that my brother warned you gives you a lot more than most folks get. Consider yourself lucky." The younger one spouted off his added warning with a slight smirk and headed off behind his brother.

Lucky? Yeah, right!

She leaned back against the wall to steady herself. Because no matter how cool and calm she might have appeared, just two interactions with Detective Hightower had her heart pounding in her chest and her knees weak. She had to catch her breath as she replayed the exchange. But most important, she had to get out of there and as far away from Detective Hightower as she possibly could.

The man screamed loud and clear without having to say a word: he could be her undoing...

"Why the hell, did you tell him her name?" Timmy glared at his twin in disgust.

"Because... Damn... It's not like it's her real name anyway. And you know what a pain in the ass Hightower can be. The man is like a bad penny. He just keeps showing up. And since we're trying to go straight now, we don't need to give him any reason to keep sniffing around."

"He doesn't need a reason. That's just his annoying way. And since we're going straight, he wouldn't find anything. And we *are* going straight." Timmy kept the threatening edge in his voice because he knew his brother had a weak will.

"I know that. But there is the issue of that jacket baby girl brought with her…" Tommy hedged.

"I got rid of it."

"You did what? Are you out of your mind? Aww dayyum."

"Now is not the time or the place. Baby girl shouldn't have been traveling with that stuff—no way. Calvin would have…man I don't even want to think about what Calvin would do if he was alive right now."

"Well, she brought it…I mean…" Tommy shrugged.

"She had no idea what she was holding."

As far as Timmy was concerned, she was still the same innocent kid he remembered from their days in California. One look at her told him that. He considered himself to be a pretty good judge of character.

"How do you know that? We haven't seen baby girl in a long time. She could have changed a lot from the kid we knew." Even though his twin argued the point, he could tell that Tommy didn't believe it, either.

Timmy shook his head. "She's still innocent and gullible and without Calvin, she's gonna need a whole lot more than us to protect her."

Tommy laughed. "Oh, I don't know. She seemed to handle Detective Hightower pretty well."

"Quiet. She's coming back." Timmy didn't say anything else because if what he suspected was true, they had a lot of trouble on their hands.

Tommy nodded. They both turned to her when she walked up. It was hard to believe the petite bombshell with the flashing, doelike brown eyes, flirty pouting smile and dimples was the same nerdy kid sister of their best friend from their youth in South Central. It was even harder to believe that Calvin was dead. Timmy knew they would do the best they could to protect her or they'd die trying. Some bonds, like the ones they shared with a friend and Crip brother like Calvin, went beyond the grave.

Lawrence returned to the table where two of his brothers, Joel and Patrick were waiting. All Hightower men shared the same trademark, Hightower good looks. They were tall, had skin in varying shades of mahogany, and rugged good looks that had been known to drive women wild.

"Dang, bro. You look like you're just waiting for one of the McKnights to so much as drop a piece of paper on the floor," Joel said, chuckling.

Lawrence glared at Joel.

Joel was the joker in the family. And he had finally regained his sense of humor after suffering a career-ending back injury, meeting and getting the love of his life to agree to marry him, and starting a new career in the family business, Hightower Security.

Lawrence tried to decide if he liked his brother better when he had lost his annoying I've-got-jokes personality. Between Joel and his woman Samantha, who also had a tendency to come up with the witty, smart-mouthed commentary, the family now had two wise-crackers in the mix.

"Just jokes, man. Lighten up. You're off duty and the McKnight twins look like they're on their best behavior tonight." Joel smiled and Lawrence knew without a doubt that his brother had been much more bearable when he had been sulking.

"What's up with the girl?" Patrick took a sip of his brew and then tilted his glass toward the table where the McKnight twins were sitting. Since his bitter divorce, Patrick was the lone member and president of the He-Man-Woman-Haters-Club. Catching his ex-wife in bed with another man had made him pretty much distrustful of the female population in general. The breakup of his marriage and an ugly divorce had left Patrick cold.

Lawrence shrugged. He didn't know. He had no clue why he couldn't take his eyes off her, either. She had a sassy mouth and looked like trouble waiting to happen. She also had the cutest face with darling dimples and a sweet, petite, and sexy body that gave her an aura of the perfect mix of innocence and sin. And she smelled like fresh-cut flowers. He wondered if it was a perfume or her natural scent.

He felt the overwhelming need to save her by getting her away from the McKnights and to lock her up and throw away the key.

She was hardly the type of woman he normally went

for. He liked them tall, shapely and pliable. So why couldn't he stop staring?

His younger brother, Jason, came back and Lawrence wondered what had taken him so long. Had he gotten any more information about Minnie Samuels?

Jason's face seemed to be on constant grin since he'd reunited with his high school sweetheart, former video dancer, Penny Keys. Marriage must really agree with him.

"Okay, you're scaring me, bro. What's the deal? Before when I found you back by the rest room, you looked like you had the girl hemmed in back there. Since when did you start giving criminals advice and helpful hints?" Jason's inquisitive gaze was all cop as he slid into the booth.

He couldn't even pretend his behavior wasn't odd. He had no idea why he'd followed her to the rest room, waited for her to come out and tried to talk some sense into her. And then for a brief moment he had thought of what it might be like to kiss her. Hell, he'd had to restrain himself from halting her mouthy retorts with his lips, his tongue and his teeth.

Lawrence shrugged, shaking off his thoughts of placing his mouth on hers. "Can we change the subject?"

"Hell, no, not now." Patrick leaned back and gave him the once-over. "You've been staring at that girl ever since they walked in. And now baby bro says she's a criminal? What's the deal?"

"I don't know what the deal is. All I know is she's

setting off my alarms. And I'm going to keep my eyes on her. And for the record, we don't know if she's a criminal. The only thing we know is she's from California and she's currently here with a couple of ex-con, gang-banger, suspected drug dealers."

"Birds of a feather, bro, *birds of a feather*." Jason took a swig of his beer.

"I don't think she's a criminal. She looks sort of sweet and maybe a little spicy... But she doesn't seem like a criminal." Joel tilted his head in contemplation.

"She may seem sweet and innocent. But she's a woman and that means she's a wolf in sheep's clothing, a barracuda." Patrick frowned.

Lawrence watched as the McKnights and the woman, Minnie Samuels, left the bar. If he didn't think his brothers would have given him a serious ribbing, he would have left, too, and followed them. But he knew his brothers. Most of all he knew what he would say to them if the situation were reversed and one of them had become suddenly obsessed with some sexy, sassy-mouthed little hood-girl.

He decided he couldn't possibly be attracted to her. He just wanted to make sure she was okay. He'd keep an eye on her until he found out more about her and figured her out. Then he'd know if she needed saving... or jailing.

Chapter 2

Detective Lawrence Hightower was a pain in her behind. He irritated her no end and she was halfway tempted to go downtown to the Paterson Police Department and file a complaint. She would have, too, but the Los Angeles Police Department was looking for her for questioning about her brother's murder. So how could she? That alone kept her from blowing the whistle on Lawrence Hightower.

It had been almost three weeks since her initial encounter with him, and she'd seen him in some capacity almost once a day for the past twenty-one days. It made no sense. He was watching her like a hawk. There had to be a rule, or a law or something…

She thought about it as she watched her clothes spin around and around at the Laundromat.

She'd been in Paterson for almost two months. The McKnight twins had a nice way of being protective and still allowing her to have her space. At first, one of them was constantly at her side. However, it became harder and harder for them to pull that off with their work schedules. The only jobs the twins could get with their records were temporary construction jobs and kitchen jobs washing dishes in restaurants. She could tell they were really trying to turn their lives around. And she felt sad that her brother hadn't been able to do the same thing before he died.

As much as she adored the McKnight twins, she was glad for the time she had to herself away from their tiny apartment and their big-brothers-always-hovering routine. Even if she had to take the time at the Laundromat, at least she had it.

"Excuse me, you wouldn't happen to have a cigarette I can borrow, would you?"

Minerva looked up to see a petite, fair-skinned woman with beautiful wavy black hair streaked with strands of gray pulled into a ponytail that hung down her back. A bright red scrunchie held the ponytail and her front tooth was chipped. She looked like she might have had a hard life at one time, but the gleam in her eyes hinted that nothing had stolen her joy. For some reason the woman made Minerva think of her own deceased mother.

"Sorry, ma'am, I don't smoke." Minerva smiled at the woman. *She seems nice enough.*

"Ma'am? Girl, please, I'm too fresh and too cool to be anybody's ma'am. My name is Carla by the way." She grinned and sat down next to Minerva. "It's good you don't smoke. It's a nasty habit. I quit smoking myself. But every now and then, I need a cigarette." She glanced over at a tall, handsome man with salt-and-pepper hair putting clothes in the machine. "This old man I got decided we aren't smoking any more *at all* and won't let me have an occasional cigarette. You believe that?" Carla rolled her eyes playfully and shrugged.

Minerva laughed. "My name is Minnie." For some reason she couldn't imagine anyone trying to tell this woman what to do.

"Girl, these men will try your patience for *real.*" Carla let out an exasperated sigh.

"You gonna just sit over there while I do all the work?" The tall, handsome man called over as he placed the coins in the machine.

"I like watching you work." Carla winked at her man.

He shook his head as he smiled.

Minerva laughed at the antics between the older couple and again she felt a pang of sadness. She tried to call up the visual image of her own parents. It was getting harder and harder to remember.

"Hello, Carla. *Minnie.*" A deep voice pulled her away from her memories.

Her heart started beating double time in her chest at the sound of his masculine baritone. She looked up to find Detective Lawrence Hightower walking into the Laundromat. Since he was not carrying any clothes and looked like he was on duty, she had the feeling the good detective wasn't there to wash a load.

"Hey! If it isn't my second favorite Hightower cop." Carla laughed. "Hey, Gerald, you better watch out. The po-po is here."

"You know him?" Minerva spared a caustic glance at the detective before turning to Carla.

"He's my son-in-law Jason's brother. He's cool people. A little too moody and he-man for my tastes, but he *a'right*."

Lawrence frowned as he stared at them and rubbed his jaw in contemplation.

"Awww…don't be mad, Hightower. You know I'm too much woman for ya anyway." Carla laughed.

"Do you know this woman, Carla?" Lawrence eyed Minerva suspiciously as he asked the question.

"Who, Minnie? Yes, this is my new girl." Carla glanced from Lawrence to Minerva. "Why you asking?"

"How well do you know her, Carla?" Lawrence leaned against the washer and folded his arms across his chest.

"Is there a problem over here?" Gerald walked over and stood in front of Lawrence. "How're you doing, Lawrence?"

Minerva's dryer stopped and she got up to get her clothes out. No way was she going to sit there and listen while the annoying Hightower cop talked about her as if she wasn't right there in front of him.

Jerk!

She emptied out her dryer and rolled her laundry cart to the back table to start folding, while mentally calling Lawrence Hightower every kind of idiot she could think of. Was the man so determined to arrest her for something, *anything?* Was he willing to provoke her until she slapped him upside the head to get her on assaulting a police officer? That must have been his plan.

As she placed her folded laundry in the big red sack she'd purchased for transport, she wished the sheets and blankets would hurry up and finish drying. She didn't bother going back up front because she could still hear Hightower's voice. She looked up when she heard him saying goodbye to Carla and Gerald. Rather than head out the door, the detective was making his way to the back.

She leaned against the table and he came and stood right in front of her. He was close enough for her to get a nice whiff of his cologne. It was one of those fresh, clean, masculine scents. The kind that made a woman think of getting swept away on an ocean. It could knock a girl off her feet if she wasn't careful, that was for sure.

Minerva inhaled and immediately regretted it.

She didn't bother saying hello. She moved her eyes from his hard-edged handsome face to the rock-solid wall of muscle that made up his chest.

"Why'd you walk away, Minnie? Did my appearance throw a wrench in your plans to try and sell your wares to Carla?"

"Go to hell."

"She says she knows you and you're her girl. But she got awfully quiet when I mentioned your relationship with known drug dealers."

She pursed her lips.

"How long are you planning to stay in Paterson, *Minnie?*"

"Why? You planning on throwing me a party, *Officer?*" She slanted her left eye and licked her lips, leaning over slightly so the little bit of cleavage she had made its presence known.

She could tell he was gritting his teeth by the pull in his jaw. His lip twitched and his eyes lost their typical suspicious stare. She licked her lips again before rolling her eyes.

"You need to stop harassing me, Detective Hightower. People might get the wrong idea and think you like me or something."

There was a pause before his lips curled into a snarl. "Anyone in their right mind would know you are certainly not my type of woman. I like them taller, shapelier and, most important, crime-free."

She felt a pain slice through her heart. No way should she have felt anything akin to hurt because the idiot cop had basically rejected her. She didn't want him to want her. She wanted him to leave her the hell alone. She gave him a once-over and noticed the considerable bulge in his pants. She might not have a lot of experience with men, but she'd kissed and made out enough times to know when a guy was getting excited. Between his bulge and his gulping for air like a fish out of water when she licked her lips, she thought maybe, *just maybe,* the detective was protesting a little too much.

She licked her lips again and watched his Adam's apple bounce. Looking up, she found his penetrating gaze zeroed in on her lips. And glancing down she found his bulge still prominent.

"Well, since I'm not your type, maybe you might want to send a memo to the rest of your body, because clearly parts of you haven't been told the news." With that she cut her eyes and walked back to the front of the Laundromat.

She eyed Carla for a moment to ascertain if the cop had poisoned the woman's mind against her. The older woman smiled and winked at her. So she retook her seat next to Carla and they both watched as Lawrence gave Gerald a pound before leaving. She had a feeling she hadn't seen the last of him for the day.

"You're not really a drug dealer, are you?" Carla asked.

"No."

Carla smiled. "I didn't think so. An old recovering addict like me can spot a dealer a mile away. And you didn't give off a dealer vibe."

"My father was a heroin addict. He died of a drug overdose, but not before infecting my mother with HIV/AIDS." Minerva had no idea why she shared that with the older woman. She didn't go around telling the world. But she felt sort of close to Carla and like she needed to say it, even if it brought home just how truly alone she was in the world at the moment.

Carla pursed her lips in contemplation. "My goodness, I'm so sorry. Well, Lawrence is right even though he is being a jackass to you. You need to watch the company you keep. A lot of messed-up stuff can happen to a young girl on these streets if she's not careful. You couldn't have told me when I was your age that I would end up addicted to crack and letting some lowlife dealer and pimp use and abuse my body. I'm blessed to have made it out. But not everyone is able to say that. Don't press your luck."

Minerva nodded. She could have gone on and on about how she wasn't going to get caught up. But something about the advice and the way it had been given told her all that wasn't necessary. She didn't have to prove herself to Carla. The woman was just being helpful.

"Whew! I've done my good deed for the week! That took a lot out of me. Ha! Hey, Gerald I think the clothes stopped. You need to put them in the dryer. I don't want to be here all day."

Gerald shook his head and went over to remove the clothes from the washer and transfer them to the dryer.

"You're off the chain, Carla!"

Carla winked. "You got to keep these dudes in check. You'll learn. So, you new to the neighborhood?"

"Yeah, I'm visiting a couple of childhood friends. I'm not sure how long I'll be here."

"That's cool."

The buzzer sounded and her sheets and blankets stopped spinning.

"It was nice meeting you." Minerva smiled at Carla before getting up.

As she rolled the laundry cart back to the tenement on Governor Street where she was staying with the McKnight twins, she hoped she wouldn't have the misfortune to run into Hightower again.

Lawrence watched Minnie Samuels struggle to pull the stuffed laundry cart up the stairs to the apartment building. It was all he could do to make himself watch and not rush over to help her with it.

Where were the idiots McKnight anyway? Why did it look like she'd been doing laundry for the entire household? And why did he care?

The hurt expression that flashed across her face when he'd said she wasn't his type came to his mind and before he knew it he was walking across the street and taking the cart from her hands. He carried it up the front steps and to the door of the McKnights' second-floor apartment.

Timmy McKnight opened the door. "Hey, girl, I was just about to go looking for you." He eyed Lawrence before turning and giving Minerva a puzzled stare.

Minerva turned to Lawrence and for a minute she looked so sweet and innocent, he just wanted to wrap her up and take her away from there. What was wrong with him? There was something about this woman that sent his emotions spiraling in all different directions.

He hadn't expected her to call him on his attraction to her. And he certainly hadn't expected her to bounce back so quickly when he'd said what he said to throw her off. But she had come back with a smart-ass comment and given him a stare that made sure he knew that she knew he'd been lying.

For her sake and his, he hoped she wasn't into anything shady. Because while it might hurt to arrest her, he would do it in a heartbeat if she proved to be a criminal.

"Thanks for your help, Detective. I appreciate it." She brushed a strand of the auburn hair from her cheek.

He couldn't believe he was finding himself attracted to a woman who had such an outrageous hairstyle.

No, he couldn't be. He *wouldn't* be.

No.

"You're welcome, Minnie." He nodded at Timothy. "Keep it clean, people. I'll be watching." He walked off just in time to hear Timothy start questioning Minerva.

"What's he—"

The rest of Timothy's words were lost to him as he left the building. But he could just imagine the conversation that was ensuing between the two of them. Maybe he should have just let her struggle with the heavy cart. But he wasn't wired that way. No Hightower worth his salt would stand by and watch a petite little thing like Minnie Samuels struggle and not reach out to help her.

He jumped into his standard-issue, navy-blue Ford Taurus narc-mobile and continued to survey and police the neighborhood. Paterson's Fourth Ward had a higher crime rate than other parts of the city. It had become so bad that the department even had little two-room trailer police stations on certain corners. He parked in front of the trailer on the corner of Straight Street and Governor and walked in.

His partner had been shot a few months ago and was still out on leave. Since Lawrence refused to work with anyone else, the top brass had essentially stopped trying to match him with a temporary new partner. That was more than fine with him. The last thing he wanted was responsibility for some young kid fresh out of the academy.

"What does it look like out there?" Johnson leaned back in his chair and rested his hands behind his head. The overweight officer took lounging to a new level.

"Same ol', same ol'. It's pretty quiet." Lawrence cut his eyes at the empty doughnut boxes and spilled coffee on the desk Johnson was using.

Cops like Johnson gave the police a bad name. The pudgy, sloppy man was a walking, talking stereotype right down to his barely concealed racism.

"You still keeping an eye on the McKnights?" Johnson brushed his hand across his beard and doughnut crumbs came tumbling off.

"Yep. Them and every other known drug dealer."

"You find out any more information about that little hottie who's been staying with them? I sure would like to break off a piece of that." The leer in Johnson's voice caused the hair to stand up on the back of Lawrence's neck.

The blood in his veins ran hot. He never really liked

Johnson anyway, and he liked him a whole lot less at that moment. He could feel the area around his neck heating to a slow boil as he tried to talk himself out of giving Johnson a piece of his mind.

The fact of the matter was he had no business caring what anyone said about Minnie Samuels. The only thing he needed to be concerned with was if she was indeed involved in any illegal activities. Barring that, he shouldn't have had any thoughts about her one way or the other. However, her voice suggesting someone needed to send a memo to the rest of his body came to his mind, and his heart thumped rapidly just thinking about her.

Pushing it to the back of his mind, he shrugged. "Something tells me you're not her type, Johnson. And I don't think it would bode well for you to try anything. Now, if you'll excuse me, some of us have work to do."

He walked to the back room of the trailer and sat down. Eventually, something would have to give as far as Minnie Samuels was concerned.

After putting away her clothes and making up the beds with the fresh linens, Minerva walked into the small, sparsely furnished living room where Timmy and Tommy were busy playing Grand Theft Auto IV. She reasoned they could have probably purchased a decent living room set with the money they had spent on electronic games, stereos and televisions. But clearly that wasn't a priority for them. And she didn't have the right to complain. They had opened up their small apartment to her when they hadn't seen her in years.

"So what was up with you and Hightower? You have to be careful with him, baby girl. He's like a pit bull. And he can sniff out crime like McGruff the damn crime dog, you hear me?" Timmy barely glanced at her as he maneuvered the control in his hands, trying to beat his brother at the video game.

"You don't want to be spending too much time around him, especially if you're trying to lay low." Tommy turned and gave her a serious stare before getting right back into the game too late to keep Timmy from scoring.

"I know that. Believe me I know. He just keeps showing up. If I weren't trying to hide out, I would file a complaint. I'm surprised you guys haven't filed a complaint yet. He really seems to have it in for you."

"He's been on us since we moved here a few years back. He's like a one-man crusade to clean up the streets of Paterson and get rid of all the dealers. Sucker needs a hobby." Timmy shouted when he scored.

Tommy scowled at his twin before adding, "The man needs a hug." He then laughed at his own joke.

"Maybe that's why he's sniffing behind you like that, baby girl. For real, if your brother were here, he'd bust a cap in that ass on general principle. Calvin didn't like *nobody* tryin' to holla at his baby sister." Timmy shook his head at the memory.

"Word. I remember he stepped to David like *whoa* a couple of times for trying to push up on her." Tommy let out a shout of glee when he scored.

Timmy gave Tommy a weird look and Tommy started stuttering and backtracking.

"I'm s-s-ay-ing…I mean…well everybody knows David had a thing for her… But Calvin didn't want his sister—" Tommy cut himself off.

"Man, it wasn't even all like that. You always running your mouth and not thinking." Timmy rolled his eyes in disgust.

"I think Timmy is right on this one, Tommy. I don't think David liked me like that. At least not as far as I could tell… He was always like a second older brother."

"Yeah. And now you've got us. And we aren't about to let anyone take advantage of you, especially not some sucker cop like Hightower. We have to handle this the way we know our boy Calvin would have wanted it," Timmy said with a chuckle.

"Y'all are so crazy. I'm gonna go read a book. I'll fix dinner later. Any requests for the chicken?"

"Baby girl, however you prepare it is fine with me. You can cook your behind off. If I didn't view you as a little sister, I'd be trying to get you to marry a brother!" Tommy gave one of his smiles that made her think he was as sweet and innocent as he often seemed. It was easy to see he was the tenderhearted twin.

Timmy rolled his eyes at his brother. "Whatever you do is cool. We appreciate all you've been doing around here."

"It's the least I can do since you've let me hide out here. I know it's an inconvenience. And I—"

"Don't even say it. Like we said before. We've got

your back," Timmy admonished and assured her with a stern words and an earnest look.

Tommy nodded in agreement as he scored the winning point and then stood up to do his own version of a victory dance.

Minerva smiled and went to the back of the apartment where the small room she was sleeping in was located. She really did want to find a way to pay them back for all the help they'd given her. She hoped to be able to do so soon. She picked up the paperback copy of Octavia Butler's *Wild Seed* that she'd gotten from the library and started reading. About halfway through she started to doze off with thoughts of the sexy detective in her head.

"I was totally wrong about you and I apologize." His hand brushed her cheek and his normally suspicious eyes held her in a seductive gaze.

Minerva leaned forward and parted her lips slightly. Lawrence looked so handsome standing there in her immaculate dream bedroom with his shirt off. The ripples of muscles she could only imagine so far reminded her of everything hard and firm and masculine.

She licked her lips and smiled. "It's okay. You didn't know any better."

"But I should have. I shouldn't have jumped to conclusions about you. You're an amazing, sweet and seductive woman and…"

She swallowed. "And…"

"And…" He covered her mouth with his, scorching her to her soul.

She wrapped her arms around his neck and pulled him closer before letting her fingers trail his skin. The taut and tempting muscles of his chest caused her heart to beat out of control. The teasing pull of his kiss made her nipples tighten and her sex weep. She moaned and tossed and turned trying to feel more of him.

"I should have known you would taste this sweet. You are the most amazing woman in the world and I want you."

The next moan that escaped her lips was so loud it jolted her from her sleep.

Minerva sat up in the bed shaking her head. Detective Lawrence Hightower admitting he was wrong about her *had* to be a dream. Him kissing her breath away was truly a fantasy. But she couldn't help the smile that stole across her face as she thought about becoming one of those people who believed dreams and fantasies could come true.

Chapter 3

"Nothing is going to happen. Nothing has happened. Nothing will happen. I'll probably be able to go back to California soon." Minerva mumbled the mantra to herself as she walked back from the corner bodega that was three blocks away from their tenement with some seasonings and spices she had picked up to use with dinner.

I love fall. I'll miss it when I get back to California. Which will be soon, because nothing has happened and nothing will...

After another week in New Jersey, over two months in all, she was starting to feel like a native. The fall came in with a bang and soon all the leaves on the trees in the neighborhood started turning these vibrant colors. She'd never seen anything like it growing up in Los Angeles. She'd seen pictures of fall foliage, but nothing could take the place of the yellows, oranges, rusts, browns and smatterings of green that transformed the trees. And it wasn't as if there were a whole lot of trees in the neighborhood where she was hiding out, but what few there were looked magnificent.

She was shocked out of her leaf gazing when a large white van screeched up, driving halfway onto the sidewalk. Two men in masks jumped out and ran toward her.

One grabbed her and, as if she were on automatic pilot, she kicked back with her stiletto-heeled boots getting him first in the shin and then a little further up his leg. She assumed she must have hit her mark by the way he threw her forward and cursed. *You can take the girl out of the 'hood but not the 'hood out of the girl.*

Dropping her bag, she screamed and turned to run in the other direction, cursing the stupid snug Apple Bottom dress she was wearing and the shoe booties. She got a good sprint on. But she knew in her heart there was no way she was going to be able to escape these men.

Her heart raced and she felt fear setting in. Fear like the kind she felt the night her brother was murdered. Was it her turn now?

I don't wanna die yet. I can't die yet.

Minerva turned to look behind her and found the other man that she hadn't injured with her heel was almost within grabbing distance.

He reached out his hand to get her and she screamed.

Her pulse seemed to be running nonstop. The air was starting to disappear and she knew she wasn't going to be able to outrun them.

Thinking there was no way she could allow herself to go out like this, she picked up the pace, only to run smack-dab into what felt like a wall of steel. A strong arm held her in place and she looked up expecting to see another masked man.

She had never been happier to see Detective Lawrence Hightower in all her life. He held her with one hand and his gun with the other.

The men didn't hesitate to take off, running back to their van. They jumped in and Lawrence ran after them, but he didn't catch them.

Her breath came out in sharp pants and no matter how much she wanted to sob, she willed herself not to cry. She stared unblinkingly at the moving van until it turned into a blur.

They must have found her. She had to leave. But where could she go?

Lawrence walked back toward her, putting his gun in his holster.

"What was that about and why were those men after you?"

Minerva's chest constricted and she tried to remember that she didn't have asthma, so she couldn't possibly be having an asthma attack. She also reminded herself there was no way she could tell the detective why the men were after her. She may not know whom she could trust, but history pretty much dictated that she couldn't trust cops.

"I don't know. That was so weird. They just came out of nowhere. Oh, my God!"

He frowned as he eyed her suspiciously. "You don't know? You have no idea? Do I look stupid to you?"

She pursed her lips and narrowed her eye.

The man *did* just save her life. She figured she should probably hold off on outright insults for at least a day or two. But he didn't have to make it so easy and tempting. She was only human, so she could *barely* keep a flip comment from falling out of her mouth.

Her expression must have given away everything she wanted to say, because he really frowned then and took her arm, leading her to his navy-blue Ford Taurus.

"Hey, what are you doing?"

"We're going to go and file a report at the trailer and you're going to tell me the truth."

"I told you I don't know. Why is it you never believe a word I say? You don't know me. You have no reason to be so distrustful of me." She tried to pull away, but he easily guided her into the backseat of the car and shut the door. She didn't even bother to try to open it because she'd seen enough movies and heard enough stories from her brother and his boys to know that back doors of police cars didn't open from the inside.

She sat and listened while he called in the details and requested officers to remain on the lookout for the white van. The entire time she listened to him speaking on the radio she tried to figure out what she was going to say. She couldn't tell him the truth and she wasn't sure she could just look him in the face and tell an outright lie.

Minerva nibbled her lips. The truth was, although she had some idea that her brother's killers were after her, she didn't know who they were. And even though she could assume they wanted her because they thought she knew something about the murder, she had no way of knowing anything with certainty.

"I think you're wasting your time," she said. "I saw the same thing you saw—men in masks. I didn't even have time to try to get the plates." She swallowed to calm herself. "As soon as they pulled up all crazy, I took off running."

"They didn't have any plates on the van. And I don't think I'm wasting my time by trying to get you to tell me the truth. Something's up with you. And I plan on finding out what it is. Folks don't roll up trying to snatch someone in broad daylight in the 'hood for no reason."

"And you know this because you have a handbook of 101 reasons to attempt a kidnapping in the 'hood or would that be the 101 reasons why people don't snatch folks in the middle of the day in the 'hood? Or could it be because you are king of all the reasons why people would do *anything* at all?"

"That smart-ass mouth is really going to get you in trouble one day. I suggest you think about that long and hard before we get to the trailer."

It didn't take them long to get to the trailer in the heart of the 'hood. She couldn't help but roll her eyes.

The Paterson Police Department seemed to be walking a thin line between *policing* and *police state*, in her opinion. Sure, it wasn't the equivalent of the constantly flying helicopters, or ghetto birds, as they affectionately called them in South Central. But mini-police huts in the 'hood seemed just a bit over the top. Whatever happened to just driving through and heading on back downtown? It wasn't like their presence really inhibited crime. All it did was ensure that she could never get away from the annoying detective.

She followed him into the trailer, happy that she wasn't in handcuffs or anything. She had had that experience once in her life and she *never* wanted to go through that again.

"Hey, Hightower. What ya got for me?" A fat man with a mustache full of food eyed her up and down as he spoke. He had a stringy and greasy flap of hair pulled from one side of his big head to the other, trying to cover up a rather large bald spot.

"Not a thing, Johnson. I'm just going to question Ms. Samuels here about an attempted kidnapping."

"There was an attempted kidnapping? Who almost got snatched?"

"Ms. Samuels."

"Really." The fat man looked her up and down.

She frowned because his survey clearly had a leering quality to it. The man gave her the creeps.

"We can talk back here, Ms. Samuels."

Minerva followed Lawrence to the back of the trailer to a relatively small room with a large desk. There were two chairs in the room, one comfortable cushioned chair behind the desk and one hard wooden one. As she took the wooden seat in front of the desk she prepared herself to lie. There was no way she could tell him the truth. That wasn't even an option, especially if someone had sent people after her when she hadn't even spoken to the cops yet.

He took his seat behind the desk and eyed her warily. "So who were those people and why were they trying to snatch you up?"

"I don't know and I don't know."

Not exactly a lie, per se.

She folded her arms across her chest and bit the inside of her cheek.

Please let that be enough for Officer Work-My-Nerves.

Lawrence shook his head. Why did he even bother? The woman was lying. A blind man could see that. Here he was trying to help the little idiot and she was content to just sit there and tell a bald-faced lie.

He gritted his teeth and pulled the collar on his knit shirt so it stretched slightly away from his suddenly heated neck.

"I'm trying to help you." He bit his words out through clenched teeth and noticed her back straighten.

"Did I ask for your help?"

"Well, considering you would have been on your way to God knows where to be raped, tortured, murdered or God knows what if I hadn't showed up—"

"You mean if you hadn't been stalking me to make sure I didn't commit some crime—"

"Watch it, Ms. Samuels. You're treading on thin ice."

Her lips twisted to the side and she shook her head.

"Were they enemies of the McKnight twins? Are they dealing again? Was the attempted kidnapping drug-related?" He fired off his questions one after the other, all the while keeping his eyes pinned on her.

She let her eyes roll toward the ceiling before cutting them at him.

"Or were they enemies of yours? You never did tell me what brings you to these parts, Ms. Samuels. Are you planning on making the Garden State your home now?"

She blinked. Her eyes shifted from side to side and she tried not to squirm in her seat.

Yep. Lying. "I have all day. Ms. Samuels." He leaned back in his chair and waited.

Her eyes snapped open. "Well, I don't."

"Then I suggest you start spilling. Who were those people and why were they after you?"

"Am I under arrest or something? Because I swear it feels like I'm the criminal here when you know full well I was almost the victim. I told you, I don't *know*."

"And I told *you*, I don't believe you."

She squirmed again, closed her eyes and took a deep breath. When she opened her eyes she looked him dead in his.

The depth in those huge dark brown pools almost took his breath away. Those eyes. That cute button nose. Those soft sensuous lips. Those dimples. Her face. He felt like he was drowning in a sea of beauty.

He had to move his gaze to that two-toned hair and expensive hip-hop brand clothing to remind himself who she really was. No matter how sweet, sexy and innocent she appeared, she consorted with known drug dealers. More than likely, she was one of them.

She let out a hiss of breath. "I don't know what to tell you, Detective Hightower. I can't make something up. I really don't know who those people were."

He noticed that even though she looked him in the eyes and seemed sincere, she didn't answer the rest of his questions.

Why are they after you, Minnie Samuels?

He leaned back in his chair. It was going to be a long day.

"I can't believe you kept me in that funky little trailer for over two hours trying to get information I don't have. If I had known exactly who tried to grab me, I would have told you." Minerva hissed out her words in irritation as she and the grating-but-sexy Detective Hightower made their way up the stairs.

The only thing she knew now was that she had to leave Paterson, New Jersey, because the people who had murdered her brother had found her.

"The ride home was fine. You don't have to walk me to my door, too. I know my way home."

"Just use this quiet time to try and see if all of the information you claim you don't know suddenly comes back to you." His calm, cool and collected voice would have been sexy if it weren't so damn irritating.

Jerk! His stubbornness meant she would have to explain to Timmy and Tommy yet again why she was with the detective from hell. Not to mention that she had to figure out where she was going to run to next.

When they reached the door to the apartment, it was slightly ajar. A chill slid down her spine.

No. No. No.

The silent scream echoed in her head as déjà vu took over and she braced herself.

Her blood ran cold as the sight of Timmy and Tommy's bodies, each with bullets in the center of their heads, met her gaze. She wrapped her arms around herself and took deep breaths.

Detective Hightower pulled out his gun and started racing through the apartment.

"I'm sorry. I'm so sorry," she whispered knowing the twins couldn't hear her but needing to say something.

When Lawrence came back, Minerva was still standing in the same spot willing herself not to cry. She had shed so many tears on the cross-country bus ride from California that she felt all cried out. The only people who knew her and her brother, who cared about them besides David, were dead.

They're dead because they tried to help me. I can't let anyone else be hurt because of me. What am I going to do?

The detective called in the murders and paced the room as they waited for the coroner and more police backup.

She watched him pace and tried to keep herself from

fleeing from the apartment. With more police on the way, Minerva didn't know what to do.

I can barely handle one detective. How am I going be able to dodge questions from more of them?

And how long could she keep the fact she was wanted for questioning about her brother's murder a secret now that two more murders had taken place?

"Who did this?"

The detective's harsh tone shocked her from her thoughts. She looked up and stared at Lawrence. He seemed to be studying her. Probably to see if she was going to tell him the truth.

Un-freaking-believable! "How would I know? You seem to forget I spent the entire afternoon with you in the freaking police trailer being interrogated like a criminal when I was almost a victim." She placed her hands on her hips and glared at him.

"I know where you were two hours ago. But until we establish time of death, we can't really rule you out as a suspect, can we? You seemed pretty resistant to me taking you home. What did you have to hide?" He walked up to her and stood right in front of her, as if he were daring her to answer him. "Unless you have some names to give… Of course this has to do with the people who tried to grab you earlier?"

Here we go again…

"Look, I told you I don't know!" She moved to walk away and he grabbed her arm.

She shook her arm but couldn't seem to shake his grasp. She blinked.

No. I will not cry! I will not give this man the benefit of my tears. I refuse.

He gritted his teeth and opened and closed his mouth twice before speaking. "Maybe some time downtown will help jog your memory, Ms. Samuels."

She blinked again. *No tears!* "What? You have got to be kidding me! You're going to arrest me? For what? Not knowing?"

"Right now, you were the last person to see the McKnights alive. You're a person of interest and, yes, I'm bringing you in for questioning." He let her arm go and threw up his hands as if he had no choice in the matter.

She pursed her lips and nodded her head as she studied him. He kept her gaze as if he halfway expected her to start spilling her guts.

Wait on! I have nothing to say, Detective.

The backup police and the coroner arrived at the same time. Soon the apartment was abuzz with activity.

She bit back the dread threatening to overwhelm her with a real and fierce indignation. Her eyes narrowed and her back straightened. Detective Hightower wanted to play hardball and there was nothing she could do to stop him. She stared at him and tried not to let her fear show in her eyes.

She held out her arms with a smirk. "Are you going to cuff me, Detective?"

Chapter 4

I'll get him back for this. One day, I will get him back for this!

Minerva allowed sweet, vicious thoughts of revenge to soothe her ego as she propped her feet up off the crusty floor onto the more-than-likely flea-infested mattress.

The only saving grace for her less-than-ideal situation was that she was in a cell by herself. Since it was a weeknight, she could only hope things were slow at the police precinct and she'd be able to remain in the cell alone. But something told her she wasn't going to be that lucky.

Somewhere between the ride downtown to the precinct and being fingerprinted by that Hightower hothead himself, she realized that Lady Luck must have left her high and dry a long time ago. When she came to grips with the fact that the detective was actually going through with it and holding her for "questioning," she let the venom take up residence and began to think of creative ways to get even with him.

With no one to call and no money for a lawyer, she was basically stuck there until the jerk decided to set her free. And even when he did decide to let her go, with the McKnight twins now dead like her brother, she had nowhere to go. Even David had disappeared on her.

She might have cried if she weren't so damn angry with Detective Hightower. He had no right to detain her when he knew she didn't do it. He was going to be sorry and he was going to pay. The man had no idea who he was messing with.

Lawrence tried to get the slight gleam in Minnie's eyes out of his head. The fact was somebody had tried to snatch her. His gut told him there was a connection between the attempted kidnapping and the execution-style murder of the McKnight twins. And there was no way he was going to leave her alone so she could end up dead. He was going to help her whether she liked it or not.

At least she hadn't cried. He could tell she wanted to, but she didn't. If she had started crying, he wasn't sure that he could have brought her in, fingerprinted her and placed her in that cell. Something told him that her tears would have stopped him cold.

Not good.

He shook his head and willed the computer to hurry up and give him some background on the mysterious Minnie Samuels. As much as his basic instincts demanded that he protect the woman, he also had the niggling suspicion there was way more to her than she was letting on. He just hoped it wasn't a criminal past she was hiding.

"What are you doing down here? I thought you'd basically moved into the satellite trailer in the Fourth Ward?"

He looked up to find his youngest brother, Jason. Jason was a cold case detective and the two of them were the only two of the brothers to follow in their father's footsteps and join the Paterson Police Department. The other Hightower brothers, Joel and Patrick, had followed the other Hightower tradition and become firefighters. Now their father James and brother Joel both worked at the company their father started when he retired from the police force, Hightower Security.

"And what are you doing with my cup? I swear every cup in this place and you somehow manage to always find my Pace cup." Jason eyed the blue mug that Lawrence drank his coffee out of.

Lawrence couldn't help but smirk. He'd had to search for the prized mug today, but he'd found it way in the back of the cabinet.

Jason must have taken a lot of time hiding it.

He didn't know when he'd decided to make it his personal quest to annoy his brothers by using their favorite cups or plates or taking the chair they always sat in. But he knew he liked getting a rise out of them. And none of them got as upset as Jason.

"You now, baby bro, you really shouldn't covet things. It's just a cup. *People* are more important than things. Think of how happy it makes your older brother to drink out of this cup." The grin on his face let his younger brother know he knew it was more than just a cup. "Plus, you weren't even thinking about this cup until you saw me drinking out of it. This thing was so far back in the cabinet there's no way you could use it every day."

Jason gave a rueful smile. "It's still *my* cup." He took a seat on the edge of the large metal desk where Lawrence was working.

While the computers and phones had been upgraded around the precinct, many of the furnishings could have used a remodel. The desk he'd been using all night looked like it weighed a ton and probably could have been used as a prop from one of those 1960s cop shows.

He took a slow sip. "Next time hide it better."

"I thought I did. I would take it home, but then I'd have to watch you drink from it every time you came over for a visit. That's a sickness, bro. You need to get that checked out."

"It's a quirk and you love it. Otherwise you wouldn't have gone to all that trouble to hide your little mug just for me to find."

"Yeah, so what are you doing here anyway?"

"The McKnight twins were murdered and someone tried to snatch the young woman who's been living with them, Minnie…" His voice tapered off as he caught the flash on the computer screen in front of him. He glanced at it quickly scanning the information that the print run had found.

No wonder it had taken a little longer. The information was a little deeper in her past but it looked like *Minerva Athena Jones* had a juvenile record.

"She was arrested for shoplifting when she was fifteen." He didn't even realize that he'd spoken the words out loud.

"Huh? What does that have to do with someone trying to grab her? And this is the woman who was at the happy-hours spot with the McKnight twins a few months back, right?"

"Yeah. And it appears that her name is Minerva Athena Jones instead of Minnie Samuels like they told me…unless Minnie is a nickname for Minerva and Samuels is her married name…" He shook his head. She couldn't be married. Oddly, he would rather she be a liar than be married.

"It could be her married name. You're looking at the juvenile record, right. If it was Jones when she was fifteen it could very well be Samuels now. And Minnie is a nickname for Minerva. Honestly, with a name like Minerva I can see why she goes by Minnie."

"Minerva was the Roman goddess of wisdom, warriors and poetry. It's a beautiful name."

He liked the name Minerva. It was different for a sister her age.

"Yeah…whatever…I'm just saying. She probably wasn't lying about her name. It could be her married name. Maybe she was on the run from an abusive husband and hiding out with the McKnights…"

"She's not married."

"You won't know until you do some more checking. Which I'm sure you will. Where is she now? Did you get her in protective custody?"

"Well, she's in custody, so to speak." He gave his brother the rundown of his afternoon and evening with Minerva.

Jason cracked a grin. "Man, she must be steaming!"

"What was I supposed to do? She won't talk and frankly, she was the last person to see the McKnights alive." He grabbed the forensics folder off his desk. "Although, the coroner's time of death gives her an alibi for the murders since she was with me at the time."

"Good thing you've become a tad obsessed with her, huh? She could either be kidnapped or dead right about now."

He didn't like the know-it-all smirk on Jason's face so he decided to just ignore his little wisecrack. Leaning back in his chair, he tried to figure out what Minerva was hiding. If he could figure that out, he'd be able to get her out of his system.

"Anyway, man, I don't want to keep you from all those pressing cold cases you have going on. One of them might be getting lukewarm as we speak. I'm gonna make some calls to LAPD and see what else I can find out about Ms. Minerva Jones."

"Ohhh snap, I've been dismissed. I must have struck a nerve. You used to be able to take a joke."

"Was that a joke? Ha, ha, I forgot to laugh."

Jason chuckled. "Well, I hope she doesn't have a record. Then you'd have to explain having the hots for a criminal."

"See ya later, bro."

"Oh, yeah, he's got it bad and that ain't good." Jason kept talking trash as he walked away from the desk.

Lawrence picked up the phone and dialed the Los Angeles Police Department. It was time to get some answers about Minerva Jones.

She raked her fingers through her hair and wished she could rip out the red hair extensions. She just knew something from that cruddy mattress had taken up residence in her hair.

Ewww.

She moved to scratch her arms and her torso before taking her digging fingers back to her head.

Yuk.

She couldn't believe that cop had kept her there all night. It wasn't as if she had another place to go, but she could have thought of lots of places that would have been better than this crusty cell.

She would have to burn her clothes, take a steaming hot shower and wash the glued-in extensions out of her hair. She only hoped that would get rid of any of the bugs or parasites she was sure had moved from the cot to her body. The clanging of the cell door caused her to look up and stop midscratch.

"So, *Minerva Athena Jones…* Did you sleep well?"

The detective walked into the cell with a sly smirk on his face and his arms folded across his chest. The only saving grace was his slightly bloodshot eyes and wrinkled clothes from the day before showed he hadn't gotten a good night's sleep, either.

Since he had addressed her by her real name, he must have been able to pull up something about her when he ran her fingerprints. She glared at him and scratched her head. As soon as she got out of there and got the *heebie jeebies* off her, she would plan a slow and painful demise for the detective. Right now, she just had to get out of this cruddy cell.

"So you must have pulled my juvenile record. Way to go, Detective! Although, last time I checked, getting busted for shoplifting when you were fifteen doesn't make you a murderer."

"Yeah, but boosting as possible gang initiation activity? Hmmm… What does that tell us about your relationship to the deceased, two known members of the Crips? What does that make you, *Minerva?* A Cripette? Were you here to help them build up the gang here? Were their murders gang activity gone bad?" He leaned against the cell and kept his gaze planted on her.

"I'm not in a gang. I failed my initiation. You know, getting caught and all. And once my brother found out…" She stopped herself.

This is exactly why I didn't need to be around this pit bull of a detective. It would only be a matter of time before he gets all the information I've been trying to hide.

"Your brother… That would be Calvin Jones?" He

arched his eyebrow in that annoying know-it-all way of his. "Known gang member… High-level Crip? He was recently murdered and the LAPD have been looking for you to question you about that, but you disappeared. Right?"

She would have leaned back against the wall but the fear of what might get on her if she did stopped her. She needed something to hold her up, though. That's what happened when it felt like the wind had been knocked out of you. She eyed the floor.

Was that red stuff blood? And what was that brown… *Yuk*.

She carefully rested one shoulder against the wall only bracing herself enough so that she didn't end up on the floor.

"Minerva, do you care to tell me why the McKnight twins and your brother were murdered execution-style? What are you holding back from the investigation and why are you hiding? I can't help you if you're not upfront."

"Whatever mess Calvin was in will get me killed too if they think I'm talking to the police."

"And what kind of mess was he in?"

"I don't know. All I know is these people have people inside the LAPD. I came to Jersey so that they wouldn't think I was talking. But I really don't know anything. My brother never let me in on that side of his life. When I was fifteen and almost joined the gang, that was the closest I ever came to his world. He only hit me once in my life and that was when I got arrested for trying to boost those clothes at the mall as a part of my initiation." She paused, remembering the altercation with Calvin.

To say that Calvin hit her was putting it mildly. But the detective didn't have to know all that. And she didn't really want to remember the one time her brother made her hate him. He had beat her so badly, he had left bruises and told her she got off incredibly light, considering what would have happened to her if she had actually been initiated. She shuddered at the things her brother had yelled at her as he hit her.

"I sucked at shoplifting and got caught the first time out. Calvin found out and lots of heads rolled. He didn't want me in the gang and he had enough pull to make sure I didn't try again."

And enough pull to make sure I thought twice before ever going against his wishes again.

Her brother had been a hard man. But she knew he did the things he did because he loved her. And because he wanted her to stay safe and alive.

"So you don't know who killed your brother or the McKnights?"

"If I knew, I would say. I went to my brother's apartment the night he was murdered because he was supposed to meet me for a celebration dinner and he never showed up. He wanted to celebrate his baby sister getting her BS degree. He wanted to take me to a really fancy restaurant but I wanted my favorite, chicken and waffles. I was late getting there. After waiting around awhile, I went to his place and that's when I saw that he'd been killed. There was someone still there going through his things but I never got a look at the person. I don't know who killed my brother. But I'm pretty sure that they know I'm here now and they're after me. They more than likely killed Tommy and Timmy. And it's all my fault." Her voice cracked and she inwardly cursed and told herself to keep it together.

He paused as he gave her a deep, penetrating stare. "Come on, let's go."

She followed him out of the cell and out of the police department. She had no idea where she was going to go now, but at least she was out of that horrible cell.

The brightness of the sun caused her to squint as she walked out of the building. She kept pace with the detective's long strides, trying to think of something to say. He seemed like he was in deep thought and she didn't want to interrupt him. But it would have been nice to know where they were going.

Just as she was about to open her mouth and ask him, the white van from the day before came speeding past. Luckily, Lawrence saw it before she did. Because before she could blink he had pushed her to the ground. The sound of gunshots caused her heart to stop and start again. She must have screamed because she heard a shrill voice echoing in her head. The only thing she could think was she hoped that Lawrence Hightower hadn't gotten shot trying to shield her. She couldn't take it if another person were hurt because of her. She couldn't bear it if he died.

Chapter 5

"Obviously someone is trying to kill you, Ms. Jones. And we can't help you unless you're more forthcoming." The chief of police, who was also Lawrence's second cousin, the youngest of his father's generation of Hightowers, tented his hands in front of his mouth and willed Minerva to speak with his eyes.

Lawrence glanced at Chief Kendall Hightower and then focused his attention back on Minerva.

He had been shot at numerous times in his career, but he had never in his life known such worry for another person. She could have been killed.

Why did that bother him almost more than the bullets that had zoomed past his own head?

"I don't know who's doing this." Her voiced cracked and her eyes pooled with tears.

If she did know who the people in the white van were, she was doing an excellent job of hiding it. Lawrence almost believed her.

"You do realize that if we let you go and you haven't been one hundred percent honest, then you could be the next murder victim? We can't help you if you're not honest." Kendall leaned back in his chair and slanted his eye.

"I understand that, sir. And if I knew…" A tear slipped down her face and she froze. She took a deep breath and gritted her teeth. Her hand went to her cheek and she wiped away the tear. "I don't know. I have to go. Can I please leave now?"

Kendall paused and then shook his head. "Don't go far, Ms. Jones. We might have some more questions for you once the investigation into the murder of Timothy and Thomas McKnight picks up. I know the Law of your tendency to leave the state during murder investigations… And we'd like to keep tabs on you for our colleagues in Los Angeles. They may have some questions for you concerning the murder of your brother. We're going to compare notes on the two cases and see what we come up with. So please don't go far."

She took another deep breath before nodding. There was the slightest tremor in her hands and chest. If Lawrence hadn't been watching her so closely he might have missed it. She looked like she had reached her breaking point and was hanging on by a thread. And he couldn't help but worry about what might happen to her once she left the precinct.

What if the people in the white van got her?

"Chief, if it's all right with you I'd like to take some personal time."

Where did that come from?

Minerva got up and walked out of the office. Lawrence followed her with his eyes and then turned back to his cousin.

He knew he couldn't let her get far. When the door closed, he took a sharp intake of breath. There would be no turning back after this.

"Look, Chief, someone has to look out for the girl. And I feel like there's a whole lot she isn't telling us. So, I'm going to take this time and watch her…if it's okay with you."

"You're narcotics, Lawrence. This is now a homicide investigation. It's not your beat."

Lawrence couldn't hold back his frown. He had to catch up to Minerva. He didn't have time to plead his case to Kendall. He would just have to use his sick time.

Kendall tented his hands and studied Lawrence. Kendall was in his mid-forties and straddled the line between the older Hightowers and the younger ones. There was no telling how he would play things sometimes. Most times he was really cool and laid-back. Other times, he might just as well had been one of the elders.

Lawrence hoped he was in cool mode today.

"Take the time and be careful. She's not telling us

everything she knows and the next bullet coming her way might catch you." Kendall shook his head. "And I'm not even gonna go there on your job duties and your responsibility to the badge. Keep your head, son."

"Yeah, Chief. I got it." He made a move to leave.

"And it might be good if you could get Ms. Jones to go someplace safe with you while you figure out what's going on with her. As long as she's with you we don't have to worry about her fleeing or ending up as another victim. I'm thinking James's spot up in the Poconos might be an ideal location to lay low for a minute until we figure out what's going on here."

Turning slowly, Lawrence couldn't help but smile. Yeah, his cousin the chief of police was in cool mode today. Kendall knew him like the back of his hand. The man had basically given Lawrence permission to do exactly what he was thinking of doing anyway.

The vacation home his father purchased for the family the first year his business, Hightower Security, did really well would be the perfect spot to take her.

"Yeah, Chief. That's a good idea. I'll do that."

Kendall nodded and Lawrence left.

As she left the rest room, Minerva chided herself on almost losing it in the police chief's office. Just what she needed: another dang suspicious Hightower cop on her case.

What does that family do, breed cops?

Everything was coming to a head and she realized she had nowhere to go. She couldn't go back to the

McKnights' apartment. She knew the people in the white van would be waiting for her there. But she wasn't supposed to leave the area. Although Chief Hightower's less-than-subtle suggestions wouldn't keep her there if she had any of David's money left to leave town with.

She sucked her teeth and huffed.

I'm getting tired of people treating me like a crook when I haven't done anything. I've almost been kidnapped, shot and I've spent the night in a cruddy cell. And I just lost three of the last four people on this earth who gave more than a damn about me. No wonder I almost cracked in that office. Hell, I'm just two events shy of an emotional breakdown! If anything else happens to me, I'll be lucky to just cry.

Someone grabbed her arm from behind and she swung her free arm to smack him as she spun around. Luckily, she noticed it was Lawrence and she stopped herself before connecting with his grill.

He caught her arm midair and placed it at her side. "Let's go."

"Go where?"

"You need a safe place to crash and I need to make sure you don't jet before we find out how you're connected to all this. So, I think it's best that you just come with me."

The man had to be crazy. It couldn't just be arrogance. It certainly wasn't just presumptuousness. He had to be a lunatic and out of his ever-loving mind if he thought she would go with him anywhere after he made her spend the entire afternoon cramped up in that funky little trailer office, after he harassed her with his never-ending questions and suspicion and after sleeping in a corroded cell getting the cooties from the millions of bedbugs that must have taken up residence in that mattress. Cooties she wouldn't be able to get rid of because she no longer had access to a shower.

She glared at him and snatched her arm away. "Thanks but no thanks, Detective. I've had enough of your company to last me a lifetime."

He narrowed his eyes in contemplation. "So where are you going to go, Minerva? I wouldn't advise you to go back to the McKnights'. That's the first place they'd probably look for you. And I really think you should seriously heed the chief's advice about sticking around. He can be a bit of a hardnose. I'd hate for him to think he had to lock you up again for your own good…"

Visions of the crusty cell swam in her head. If she were prone to whining and complaining in even the slightest way, she would have started stamping her feet and screaming, "*Why* me?" at that very moment. Good thing life had dealt her enough hard knocks not to expect lots of pleasant things to happen to her *just because*… But she seriously could have used a small shift in luck for a change.

He held out his hand. "Come on. Let me help you."

"Why do you want to help me?"

He paused and his face sort of twisted up. "Look, you need to decide if you want to risk it out there against folks trying to get you who *you claim* you don't know, or let me help you." He turned and started walking in the opposite direction.

She stood there for a few seconds and then shrugged. No good could come from hanging around the detective too long no matter what he said. He would probably find some way to pin all the murders on her and convince the world that she was really Bin Laden. No, she needed to keep it moving. She turned and kept walking.

Now, if I can just figure out— "Whoa!" She screeched as her thought processes were interrupted suddenly. Just as she made it to the front door she felt herself being lifted from the ground and before she knew it she was over Lawrence's shoulders.

"Put me down, Lawrence Hightower! This is kidnapping and we're in a freaking police station!"

"Shut up, Minerva," he said in the calmest voice she'd ever heard.

They headed out a side door and down some stairs to an underground parking garage. When he finally put her down in front of a black SUV, she straightened her dress and contemplated running off again.

"Don't even think about it, Minerva." He opened the door and nodded for her to get in. Her name rolled off his lips with a hint of a threat but there was something else underneath.

A hint of sexiness? Seduction? What the heck was it about the way this man says my name that gives me the chills? I'm talking sweet, achy, makes me feel so good chills… The way Lawrence said her name could make her grow to like, hell even love, the quirky name.

She folded her arms across her chest and stood there.

"Get in."

Who did he think he was? Just because he saved her life a couple of times did not mean he was all of a sudden in charge of her. The last time she checked she was a grown-ass woman. However, as grown as she was, the only thing she could think of to do was stamp her feet and yell that he was not the boss of her.

Real mature…

She bit back a huff and got into the SUV. At the end of the day, she didn't have anywhere else to go and as annoying as the overbearing detective was, he seemed to be the only thing between her and danger. She wasn't one of those too-stupid-to-live chicks in the movies who went looking for danger or turned down help when she needed it.

She decided: she had to stop fighting him, but she didn't have to like it.

Chapter 6

So she was just going to sit there and not say a word to him the entire ride?

Well, fine.

Lawrence wasn't about to beg her to talk to him. In fact, if she was going to make one of her little smart-ass comments or tell one of her lies, or try and convince him that she really didn't know who was after her, then he would rather she not say a word.

Yeah. He could deal with the silence. It would give him plenty of time to think about what it was about this woman that had him going against all his normal reflexes. Why was it that merely seeing her made him want to pull her in his arms and see how those sweet pouting lips of hers tasted? Or how come he had an almost instinctual desire to protect her and look out for her? And darn if his desire for her wasn't making him…

No, to hell with silence!

He did not need to face those questions yet. And besides, they might go away.

Or maybe they weren't really all he was making them out to be.

Just as he reached to turn up the radio, they lost the station. It was the only thing he hated about the drive to the Poconos. About forty minutes into the drive down Interstate-80 the good radio stations were gone. He flipped the CD changer on and darn if everything he had in it wasn't slow and smooth R & B. He certainly didn't need mood music, so he turned it off.

She was just going to have to talk to him.

"Why are you being so quiet?"

She didn't say anything.

"You know, believe it or not there are lots of other things I could be doing with my time rather than trying to look out for a ungrateful chick who may or may not be telling the truth."

A suck and a hiss was her only response.

"Minerva…" He paused when he sensed that she had turned to face him. He stole a quick glance and found her eyes pinned on him. "Minerva, this will go a lot easier if we at least try to get along. I'm really not that bad of a guy once you get to know me. And I would really like to get to know the truth about you. So why don't we try—"

"What makes you think there is anything more to

know about me? You found out about my juvie record. You know about my brother's murder. You have been a freaking shadow in my life for the past three months. You know that there are people after me—"

"Yeah, but I don't know who is trying to get you—"

"Neither do I! Why don't you believe me? You don't even know me and yet you have painted me as some kind of lying crook. I resent that. I resent you. And I refuse to keep trying to convince you that I'm innocent. If we can't find anything else to talk about then I'd prefer silence."

Well, damn. It was like a gust of wind when she turned back around to face her window.

So, no talking for now…

But she would have to talk to him soon. He swallowed and focused on the drive.

They would have to stop in Tannersville at the outlet mall. He didn't stop to get any of his clothes and he certainly wasn't going to risk picking up her things from the McKnights' apartment. So they would both need to pick up some items for the duration. She looked like the kind of woman who liked to shop. Maybe that would put her in a better mood. If not, this would be the longest and most painful time he had ever spent with a woman.

She tried to curb her irritation. She really did. But the last thing she felt like doing was trying on clothes and shopping when she still felt like she had a billion bedbugs creepy-crawling on her skin. As much as she loved a sale, she wanted a hot shower! As she looked through the sale racks in the Dress Barn outlet all she wanted to do was wash the bright auburn weave tracks out of her hair because she knew the critters must have been harvesting and hashing in it

Pretty much forgetting her alias identity and the hip-hop clothing she'd been wearing, she opted for the business and relaxed casual style she was most comfortable in. The little disguise hadn't worked anyway. They still found her and the Baby Phat minidress she was wearing was working her last nerve, rising up and what not. She hoped she'd be able to burn the thing later. It was probably infested anyway.

Once she'd found a few outfits, shoes, a nightgown and some underwear in clearance, she went up to the cash register. It was then she realized that she didn't have any cash on her but she did have her credit cards and debit card. She had been afraid to use them before because David hinted that the police or the people who had killed her brother might be able to trace her if she used them. But the crooks had found her and she was stuck with a cop, so she might as well use her cards.

"I got this." Lawrence stepped up and pulled out his credit card.

"You don't have to. I can pay my own way."

"You sure? It's not a problem for me to handle it. In fact I insist." He gave the cashier his credit card.

She could have made a big scene but realized it was

unnecessary. As controlling and unyielding as he seemed to be, he *was* trying to keep her safe.

Once they picked up a few items from a men's store for him, they ended up in a beauty supply shop. She needed the special shampoo to get rid of the glue that held the weave in her hair. And she couldn't wait to get rid of it. She also needed a blow dryer and curling iron if she wanted to make her natural curls manageable.

As he opened the door to the SUV for her to get in, she paused in front of him. He looked so handsome and stoic and purposeful. She pursed her lips and crossed her hands behind her back.

"Thanks, Lawrence. For everything."

He leaned down and placed his forehead on hers. The closeness would have had her gasping for air if she wasn't forcing herself to remain composed.

Oh, my goodness…

"I'm not going to let anything happen to you. I promise you that." His lips brushed her forehead and she wished he had kissed her.

The hot feel of his lips with just that featherlike touch made it feel like she had firecrackers in her socks. She swallowed back her groan and got into the SUV before she was tempted to grab his head and thrust her tongue down his throat.

They drove the rest of the way in silence. She felt a little bad about not speaking. But she had to resist him in any small way she could. Just because he wanted to talk did not mean she *had* to talk. He didn't believe a word that came out of her mouth, anyway. Sure, she would have welcomed the distraction of conversation if it would have taken her mind off how sexy he was, even when he was sitting there brooding. But, unfortunately, his voice did something to her, especially the way her full name rolled off his tongue.

Nope, he didn't have to say a word.

The landscape along the way sort of took her mind off the big, powerful cop driving. She took in the fall foliage along the Pennsylvania highway as they made their way down I-80. Fall would always be her favorite time of year now that she saw what a real fall looked like. Who knew nature could look so beautiful when it was dying? The mix of gold, rust, red, orange and specks of green took her breath away. The entire drive had been so scenic. Once they made it about twenty minutes away from Paterson, she started to see why they called New Jersey the Garden State.

After a little over two hours on the road, they arrived at their destination. The home was beautiful. It looked like something she'd seen on HGTV. The huge white house with yellow shutters had two stories. It had a wraparound porch with stacks of wood and even a couple of wooden rocking chairs.

"This my family's vacation home. My dad bought it a few years back when the security company he started after retiring early from the police department started to do really well. Hightower Security is now the leading security company in the East." He paused and ran his hand across his head. "The family tries to get up here in the winter for some skiing and just hanging."

Vacation home? Skiing? Good grief!

She knew her jaw must have been on the floor. Because her family had never owned a *home* let alone a vacation home. Add that to the fact that she didn't even have family anymore and she got all the more reason why she needed to get over her growing infatuation with the detective. He was way out of her league.

Talk about mooovin' on up, tooooo the East siiide... she sang in her head.

"I'll bring in the bags. Pick any room you'd like. I'll call the grocer and have some groceries delivered, depending on what's in the fridge and freezer... Are you okay?" He stared at her.

He must have noticed that she wasn't moving. She tried to make her feet move and pick up her jaw but the inside of the place was just as gorgeous as the outside. Warm earth tones and rugged leather and wood furniture greeted her eyes, along with amazing African-American artwork that complemented the decor. Paintings by Ed Clark, Herbert Gentry, Vannette P. Honeywood and Brenda Joysmith. Minerva recognized them from her recent art history course in college. As she took in the cozy rusts, browns and creams, she remembered to exhale the breath she'd been holding. The house had six bedrooms. Six! She picked the smallest, least intimidating bedroom in the place and even that one had its own bathroom.

When he dropped off her bags, she wasted no time

getting in the shower. Maybe once she got out of her crusty clothes and got the God-awful weave out of her hair she would feel better and more capable of standing up to the detective.

A girl could hope...

It didn't take Lawrence long to shower and get changed. There was one package of chicken legs and tons of tomatoes from his mother's garden in the freezer, but not much more. He made a call to the grocery store, which was a few miles away, to have some things delivered. His family's house was in a pretty isolated location in the Poconos. That was excellent for hiding out, but not so good when it came to getting stuff from the outside brought in. He made a mental note to call the sheriff and deputy, Dale and Jed, to let them know he was in the house and get them to help keep an eye out for the white van, just in case. They were small-town cops, but it couldn't hurt.

When the groceries were delivered and she still hadn't come out of her room, he was starting to worry. After he put the food and supplies away and there was still no sign of her, he started to get pissed. He was not going to allow her to pull that silent treatment crap the entire time. Like it or not, he was only trying to help her and she needed to get over her attitude and start showing a little appreciation.

He took off down the hall and up the stairs. Just when he was about to knock on her door it opened.

Gut-punched! That's what it felt like when he cast

his eyes on the most beautiful vision he'd ever seen. And he wasn't even expecting it.

Sucking in a big gulp of air, Lawrence felt his eyes bulge and his mouth drop when he caught a glimpse of the woman standing in the door. The two-toned hair was gone and her natural dark brown hair fell just past her shoulder in soft curls that framed her face. She wasn't wearing any makeup, just a hint of lip gloss. And she had on a pair of black wide-leg slacks with cream pinstripes and a silky, sexy cream V-neck tee that accented her cleavage nicely.

He tried to figure out how she managed to look even sexier in the smart professional clothing than she had in that skin-tight minidress she'd been wearing. And he wondered why she looked so much prettier than any other woman he had ever seen when she clearly wasn't even trying.

"Sorry I took so long. After a night in that cell, I felt like I needed to take an extra-long shower and it took a minute to get the hair together after washing those tracks out." She let her hand pass through her hair and it glided through the softness.

He wondered what she had had in her hair before besides the weave that had disguised her curls and made her hair seem so stiff. He placed his own arms behind him in an effort to stop himself from reaching out and running his fingers through her gorgeous tresses.

"I'm just glad I feel like my old self again. The long time it took was well worth it. If I never see another Baby

Phat or Apple Bottom again, I will have no problem at all."

He gulped.

He knew she was twenty-six years old from the record he pulled. But she looked about twenty-one with her face freshly scrubbed and those glossy brown curls framing her face. She looked too young for his thirty-seven-year-old self. But damn if he cared. When it came to the feelings he found himself having for Minerva, age wasn't nothing but a number.

She stared up at him and a self-conscious expression crossed her face. "I know. You probably think I look like a dweeb. But that's okay. No more multicolored weaves in my head for life." She scratched her head. "I still feel like I could wash it again."

"It looks fine." Was that him? So...he *could* talk. And here he thought her beauty had stolen his damn voice.

"What do you want for dinner? I can fix something," he managed to grumble in what sounded more like a sputter to his ears.

Maybe he should have just let her stay in her room all night. He certainly didn't need this complication. The desirable woman who stepped out of that bedroom made him want to take her back into the room and do all kinds of naughty things to her until she begged him not to stop. He licked his lips and imagined how that lip gloss might taste.

"How about I cook for us. It's the least I could do since you're being so nice and you're taking your time to help me. I'm pretty good in the kitchen and I could whip something up. Just point the way."

"You sure? You don't look like…I mean, I'm fine with cooking and I'm pretty particular about food…"

The plastered-on smile she had been wearing dropped and her eyes narrowed. She let out a breath and then bit her lower lip. He could just imagine what words she must be biting back and he would have felt like a heel if he weren't so busy wondering what it would feel like to be the one nibbling on those pouting lips.

He placed his finger on his chin as he thought about their situation. She was holding out an olive branch and he had basically grabbed it, thrown it on the ground and stomped on it. And he was lusting after her to boot. He could see that the glint in her eyes hinted that she was thinking about doing him bodily harm.

"I said I would cook something for us," she said between clenched teeth. "It's the least I can do, and I intend to do it." She offered a tight smile. "Now please point me toward the kitchen. I'm hungry and the sooner I get started the sooner we can eat."

Fine. If she wanted to cook so badly, he might as well let her. Besides, once he tasted her nasty food, he wouldn't have to worry about his attraction to her. Everyone knew his lifelong motto: The woman he would marry, who didn't exist as far as his bachelor creed was concerned, would have to be as good a cook or better than his mother.

And he hadn't dated a woman yet who could measure up.

What he couldn't figure out was why he was even thinking about her meeting his standard in the first place. Why was his mind even going there?

He frowned. "Are you sure I can trust you to make me dinner? I mean, you won't try to poison me or anything like that, will you?"

She turned and rolled her eyes. "Why don't you just watch me then, Detective, if you don't trust me?"

"I intend to, Minerva. I intend to."

He had to admit, as he observed her working in the kitchen, she certainly had the skills down pat. Even the way she cleaned the chicken, taking the time to burn off the hairs and the few stray feathers that the butcher had missed. She moved around the kitchen like a woman familiar with one. But that didn't mean the food would taste good.

It smelled pretty good cooking, though. Who was he kidding? His stomach growled and his mouth watered, the longer he sat in that kitchen watching her hum and slice and dice and move around. He figured it must be because he was hungry. That had to be it. And even if she could throw together a down-home delicious meal, there was no way she could compete with Mama's cuisine, so he was safe.

Chapter 7

Minerva watched as Lawrence ate her food. She guessed he at least found it edible because he was piling it in. He had a little system going—eat a mouthful, groan in pleasure, gaze at her in wonder, squint, frown and repeat. When he fixed a second plate, she knew he must have enjoyed the meal.

She knew she could cook. She'd been cooking since she was a kid, especially once her mother got sick. And when it was just her and Calvin, she cooked for him and his friends all the time. Once Calvin had really gotten into his illegal activities, there had always been plenty of food to eat.

What she couldn't figure out was why Lawrence seemed so aggravated. She had offered to cook because after her shower and washing her hair, she decided to try and forge a truce with the detective. As annoying as he was, she owed him a lot. And even though his reasons for following her around and keeping an eye on her were outright wrong, if he hadn't been watching her she might be dead. And having a place to lay her head—her weave- and color-free head—meant a lot.

The shower had washed away a lot of her ill feeling toward Lawrence. But his antics during the meal she had worked so hard to whip up were raising her ire again.

"Does it taste okay?"

He glanced up from his plate in irritation. "Yes."

"Why do you keep shooting me those funny looks then? If the food tastes okay, then why are you acting like that?" She felt her nostrils flare and she exhaled.

"Acting like what? I'm eating."

"Your eating like you're angry that the food is good." She tilted her head to the side as she tried to figure him out.

Maybe trying to bury the hatchet with this man was a mistake. He seemed determined to think the worst of her and genuinely disgusted when he had to change his opinion—like the expression on his face when she opened the door to her bedroom and he got a glimpse of how she normally looked, the real her. His face went from shocked to interested to peeved in a matter of minutes.

"You know, the trouble with judging people before you really know anything about them, Detective, is that most of the time you end up eating your words and coming out wrong." She pushed her plate away. Suddenly she didn't have much of an appetite. "I might not be from the same background as you. And I may not have grown up with the same advantages. But believe it or not, before my brother was murdered and my world got turned upside down I was a pretty normal girl. I went to work and school and I had plans for my future. And I can even cook. *Imagine that.*"

"So are you saying I have you pegged all wrong?"

"If you think I'm some murdering, drug-dealing criminal who can't burn in the kitchen, yes. You have me pegged *all* wrong."

His lips curled and his dark eyes sort of sparkled. Her heart jumped double Dutch, speed-jumping competition-style. She didn't think she had ever seen him smile like that.

Oh, she'd see him smirk and snarl and sneer… But smile? No. And she had no idea his eyes could be so sweet and kind and shiny. If he was fine when he was dark and brooding and suspecting, this new expression made him drop-dead gorgeous. She felt like she was about to be in trouble—deep, deep trouble.

"I don't think you're a murderer. And I will admit this meal was outstanding. You can burn with this meal. But you might be one of those one trick sistahs. You know, the ones who perfect one meal to try and nab a guy and then he finds out that's all she can cook." He laughed.

He didn't say he believed she wasn't a drug dealer.

He said he didn't think she was a murderer. She didn't know why she was so hurt by him not saying he believed in her. She also had no idea why she wanted so desperately for him to believe in her.

She swallowed as she nodded her head and tried to push back her confused feelings. "Well, since I'm *not* trying to nab a man, but just trying to be nice and hopefully forge a truce, then I guess it really doesn't matter if I'm a one-meal sistah. But, just so you know…I *can* cook more than one dish. And I'd be happy to cook for you again, since you seem to enjoy my food. But don't think I'm going to break my neck trying to prove to you I can cook. You'll have to share in some of the cooking, Detective."

He nodded with a rueful grin. "My mouth has gotten me in trouble. I was looking forward to seeing what else you can do…"

"Mmm-hmm, I'll bet you were. You almost had me ready to pull out all the stops and prove that I could cook my behind off just so that I could prove you wrong about something finally. That's at least something I could prove." She shook her head. She shouldn't care whether he believed in her or not.

"If it would make you happy to prove me wrong on this, I'm more than willing to subject myself to more of your cooking." He smiled.

A real smile.

That could be her undoing for sure.

"This fried chicken…" He paused and gave a rueful grin. "Don't ever tell anyone I said this, but this fried chicken is *better* than my mama's." He shook his head before diving back into his food.

She smiled, got up to empty her plate in an effort to start cleaning up.

"What are you doing?"

"I'm going to throw this away and start cleaning the kitchen."

"Waste not, want not. I'll take care of that. And I'll handle the cleanup since you cooked. Sit down. Finish telling me all about my judgmental self."

Her skin felt flush and heat raced to her cheeks. She had called him out, hadn't she? Goodness, she certainly sucked at the whole calling-a-truce thing.

He grinned as he scraped what was left of her potato salad, fried chicken and green peas onto his plate. "To be fair, you have to admit that your living with the McKnights gave me plenty of reason to suspect that you might be into the same kinds of things that they were into."

"Guilty by association? That hardly seems fair, Detective. And you also weren't fair to Timmy and Tommy. They were making a change and trying to do right. They weren't involved with whatever they used to be involved in. But you still rode them and judged them by their past."

"But someone killed them, Minerva. Someone shot them both execution-style."

"That doesn't mean they were guilty of anything, Detective. It means they were victims of a heinous crime."

"What was your major?"

His question threw her off track. She'd been set to make her passionate plea about how Timmy and Tommy had taken menial jobs wherever they could in order not to go back to their life of selling drugs. She hadn't been prepared for a personal turn in the discussion.

"Sociology with a double minor in women's studies and African-American studies. I hope to go back for my MS or MSW eventually and get a job in social work."

"Women's studies?" He slanted his eye and twisted his lips.

"Yes. Women's studies." She tilted her head and pursed her lips.

"So, now you want me to believe that you're a feminist?" He arched his right eyebrow.

"Womanist or hip-hop feminist, depending on what day you catch me."

"Womanist, huh?" Studying her intensely, he rubbed his chin and it made her get goose bumps up and down her arms and back. "Hmmm... Like Alice Walker... We had to read *In Search of Our Mother's Gardens* in one of my black studies electives in undergrad. But a hip-hop feminist? Now that's an oxymoron if I ever heard one."

"You have to read Joan Morgan's work, she breaks it down in her book *When Chickenheads Come Home to Roost*."

He rolled his eyes and chuckled before responding. "The title of that book alone should be the reason why hip-hop and feminism don't mix."

"You should read the book before casting *judgment,* Detective," she said with a smirk.

"Yeah, I guess so, I would have never pegged you for a womanist or a feminist with those little short dresses you were sporting around town. So I guess I do need to slow my roll when it comes to passing judgment as far as you're concerned."

She bit back her whole spiel about a woman's style of dress having no bearing on her mind or politics and her rant on societal double standards. It just stunned her speechless that he was willing to admit that he needed to be a little slower to judge her.

She blinked away the warm fuzzy feelings that threatened to overwhelm her. "So you were all in my business. What was your major in undergrad?"

"I have a bachelor's and a masters in criminology."

All those degrees and you still can't tell when someone is innocent. Wow.

Smiling, she was pleased with herself when she was able to keep the smart-mouthed comment to herself.

"Did you always want to be a cop?"

He smiled softly and shook his head. She realized she could easily get used to his smile.

"My family is full of cops and firemen. The men in my family have just historically gravitated toward one or the other. And when I was growing up, I was the one Hightower who had decided he wanted to rebel. I pretty much pushed all the limits until…until someone I thought was my friend showed his true colors and I got a wake-up call about how fragile life really is. From that point on, I knew that no matter how much I had resisted the family legacy, I had a calling and that calling was to fight crime and rid the streets of drugs."

She nodded. She could appreciate his calling and even admire it.

"As much as I don't trust cops, I have to say that's an honorable calling, Lawrence. I lost both my parents to my father's addiction. The only thing I can hope is that my brother really held true to his vow never to sell drugs because of what heroin did to our family. And even though I know it'll take more than me saying it for you to believe me, I would *never* sell drugs." She closed her eyes and thought about stopping. She had no idea why she felt this overwhelming need to share this part of herself with the detective. But she had to.

"I'm not a drug dealer. And no matter how badly I needed a place to hide out from my brother's killers, I wouldn't have spent three months under Timmy and Tommy's roof if they had been selling drugs. Watching your mother waste away from AIDS because she loved a man who didn't love himself enough to kick the habit or at least get a clean needle was enough to turn me off drugs for life."

Lawrence swallowed and nodded. He hadn't said he believed her. And Minerva supposed she should have just left it at that. She couldn't make him believe her, no matter how much she desired it. No matter how much she desired him… And she was willing to admit that she desired him. She just had no idea what to do about it.

"Well, I guess that's enough getting to know you for one evening."

"Ya think?" She giggled, relishing the easy sound. Was she starting to become comfortable with this detective? Lord help her if she was.

She helped him clean up, even though he said she didn't have to. They set an easy pace, him washing and her drying. And once they were done she turned to head to bed.

"Minerva." Her name on his lips just sounded right.

"I like the way you say my name. It almost makes me like it more." She realized she'd spoken the words out loud before she had a chance to stop herself.

He leaned against the sink and studied her. "It's a beautiful name—the virgin goddess of wisdom, warriors, poetry and crafts. But twice—Minerva and Athena?"

She felt her cheeks heating up just from the way he was staring at her. They really heated up when he said the meaning of her name, especially the virgin part. If only he knew…

"My mother had a serious thing for Greek and Roman gods and goddesses—go figure. I guess my mother wanted to be sure I'd be smart and could handle myself in the world. I normally go by M. Athena or Thena."

He smiled. "Well, I'm going to call you Minerva."

As she thought about what it would sound like if he said it again and again, over and over, he said it again.

"Minerva, thanks for the delicious meal. And thanks

for sharing a little bit about yourself with me." His arms folded around her.

The embrace seemed as if it had started out as quick thank-you hug. But something happened… If Lawrence felt anything like the thousands of tingles that were coursing through Minerva's body and dancing across her skin, then she was surprised he could still stand. If he hadn't been holding on to her and giving her a good whiff of his cologne, her knees would have buckled. His arms tightened and hers wrapped around him, too, giving him a long squeeze.

He felt so magnificent, so hard and solid. And her heart wouldn't stop pounding.

He brushed his lips across her forehead again and she groaned, wishing his lips had touched hers.

"I'm going to help you. I'm not going to let them get you."

She just nodded. What could she say? She wanted his help and she was finally ready to accept it. She just hoped that neither one of them ended up sorry about that.

Chapter 8

After tossing and turning the entire night, waking up to the smell of coffee perking and breakfast cooking put more pep in Lawrence's step then he could have garnered otherwise. He walked into the kitchen and found Minerva hard at work. The hickory sweet aroma of bacon wafted past his nose as he poured a cup of coffee.

She flipped the pancakes on the griddle and hummed as she cooked.

He blinked. Her springy curls were cascading around her face in a soft, seductive frame. She had on a pair of sexy, form-fitting jeans and a scoop-neck red tunic that brought out the wonderful undertones in her skin and made her appear even more perky and dynamic. The jeans caressed her bottom snuggly, the way he wanted his hands to. She wore red socks on her feet and nothing else. He wondered what her toes looked like.

The sun shined brightly through the windows and seemed to pop off the yellow-and-white gingham wall-paper on the walls. Everything looked perfect as far as his eyes could see. He tried to figure out if the normally homey kitchen felt even more so because of her presence.

He shook his head and pushed away the thought before he could answer it. He knew he wasn't ready for the answer.

"I hope you like cinnamon-apple pancakes."

"We had pancake mix?"

She tilted her head sideways. "No…but you had all the ingredients I needed to make a batter."

"From scratch?" Not many women—hell not many people—these days made anything from scratch. His rubbed his chin as he tried to figure out the woman standing in front of him.

She rolled her eyes and took the pancakes off the griddle. "I should have eaten my food last night. I'm starving."

"Me, too." He grabbed the plates and silverware.

They fixed their plates and sat down to eat. As he ate her delicious food yet again, he marveled that Minerva Jones was going to have him eating his words, at least when it came to her cooking.

"This is good!" He couldn't hold back the praise. It was still bubbling over from last night's meal. "Listen,

I'm sorry, I was tripping last night. You are no joke in the kitchen, baby. I was just playing around when I said that stuff about you being a one-dish girl. And we both know that, as pretty as you are, you don't have to resort to trickery or anything like that to nab a man."

Yes, he was laying it on thick. But anyone who knew him knew he loved a well-cooked, homemade meal. He wanted to see what else she could do in the kitchen, and he also needed to get back on her good side. How could he get what he desired if she continued to think he was a jerk?

A perplexed expression crossed her face for a moment and then she frowned. Twisting up her lips, she smirked. "Uh-uh…no need to try and gas me up. You're still taking over your fair share of the cooking."

"But we're onto something good here. Something beautiful…where you cook these delightful meals and I eat them and tell you how wonderful you are. Win-win."

"Nah. That's okay. I'll pass. We can take turns." She grinned at him and he felt like he'd been gut-punched again.

"So what do you want to do today?"

"I don't know. Is there a lot to do here?"

"Well, the ski season hasn't started yet, so not really. But we can take a walk later. Enjoy nature. Take in the scenery. I don't want to venture off too far and I'd like to stay away from public places, just in case the folks who're after you show up."

"You think they'll show up here?"

"No. They shouldn't. I didn't see anyone following us. We should be cool. But there's no need to tempt fate. So it's just you and me for a few days, Minerva. You think you can handle that?" He smiled at her and tried not to think about the fact he'd been doing a lot of that lately. He was surprised his mouth hadn't gone into shock.

"Sure I can. Can you?" She tilted her head in a daring manner and he wanted to pull her into his arms and kiss that smirking mouth.

"Oh, I can handle it, sweetheart. I can handle it just fine." He kept his eyes pinned on her and she held his stare.

She swallowed and blinked before turning away. "Should we clean up the kitchen?"

"I'll get it since you cooked. That's another benefit of cooking, sweetheart. I'll handle the cleanup so you won't have to get any dish detergent on those soft pretty hands of yours…"

She busted out laughing. "You're reaching now, Lawrence."

He chuckled. "Hey, I have to try. My stomach and taste buds are cussing me out because of my big mouth. Please cook for me again, pretty baby, please."

She leaned over and cracked up. When she sat back up after busting a gut, she had laugh tears in her eyes. She stood. "Wow, you are funny, Detective. I had no idea you were this funny. Thanks for the laugh. I'm going to get one of the books in the den to read. I can't wait to go for a walk with you later, Lawrence." She smiled softly before leaving him.

He tried not to read too much into her sweet glance. But how could he not? He wanted her and he wanted her to want him, too.

She'd tried extremely hard to just lose herself in the Toni Morrison novel she had gotten from the bookshelf in the den. She usually loved Morrison's work. She'd taken a contemporary black authors class a few semesters back and had read *Beloved* and *Sula*. Both had been rigorous reads, but well worth the struggle. She was pleased to see the full Morrison collection among the books on the shelf.

She loved to read and tried to concentrate but she kept seeing Lawrence's smiling face and sparkling eyes. She would have never thought those dark and dangerous eyes could shimmer and shine so much. He seemed like an entirely different person, one she wanted desperately to get to know, among other things…

When he came to get her for their walk, she was more than ready and more than a little anxious. They walked in silence for several minutes and she just took in the breathtaking sights. She had never seen so many trees.

Some of the leaves had started falling and brown leaves covered the ground. The trail they followed got steeper and she realized they were walking uphill. They didn't call it the Pocono Mountains for nothing. She was glad she'd had the foresight to purchase a pair of sensible shoes while they were at the outlet mall. Those stiletto-heeled boot-shoes she'd been wearing while she lived with the McKnights wouldn't have made it.

"So what did you say you are you planning on doing with your degree in sociology?" His rich melodious voice pulled her from her thoughts.

"I hope to go to graduate school and get my MSW. I want to work with at-risk youth and hopefully run a youth center one day. I'd love to be able to make sure that fewer kids got involved with gangs and drugs, help them see other options."

"That can be kinda dangerous work, Minerva."

"Not as dangerous as your job."

"Yes, but I'm a—"

"You're a what? *A man?* I know—"

"Hold on a minute little womanist *slash* hip-hop feminist. I was going to say, I'm a cop. I'm trained to work in these environments, to clean up the streets."

"And as a social worker, I'd be trained to work with people to make sure the streets get a little less dirty from the get-go. Someone has to make sure that the young people have other options and don't end up filling the jail cells."

"Yes…but does it have to be you?"

What did he mean by that?

She stopped in her tracks and put her hands on her hips.

He walked a couple of paces before stopping. "What happened? Are you okay? Are you tired? You wanna head back to the house?"

She could feel the heat of anger rising from her neck

and coming out of her ears. She tried to tell herself to calm down. It didn't work.

"What is your problem? You don't think I'm good enough to work with kids?"

"What are you talking about?"

"'Does it have to be you?'" She mimicked his judgmental voice.

He tilted his head and scrunched up his brow. Taking two steps toward her, he pulled her to him when he reached her. She hadn't been expecting it.

She fell into his arms with very little resistance. He wrapped his arms around her and she let out a soft hiss of breath. He used one of his hands to lift her chin and peered in her eyes.

Lawd in heaven, mercy mercy me...

"I asked does it have to be you because for some reason the idea of you in danger doesn't sit well with me. From the first moment I laid eyes on you hanging with the McKnights, I have been trying in my own... way...to remove you from danger..." He had this intense expression on his face, this perplexed look in his eyes like he was trying his best to figure something out.

"Oh..." was the only thing she could think of to say.

"Yeah...oh..." He smiled before his mouth swooped down and covered hers.

Hot. Searing. Passion.

She opened her mouth and an explosion of sensation and desire knocked down any resistance she might have had. She'd never tasted anything as delicious as Lawrence's lips, his tongue. The man's mouth relentlessly plundered hers, sucking, licking, nipping and devouring. It was all she could do to try to keep up and give as good as she got.

And she got a lot.

Her body tingled. Waves and ripples of pleasure traveled from her mouth to her core. He picked her up and walked toward a soft spot on the ground under a tree where the fallen leaves had made a nice cushion. He placed her down and followed, pinning her between the earth and himself, all the while continuing his raid of her mouth.

His tongue twirled and teased and tempted but never relented. Her tongue danced and relished the flavor of his talented mouth. She ran her tongue past the roof of his mouth, pointing and pulsing. She licked his lips and savored.

No, she hadn't kissed a lot of men in the past, and after getting a dose of what Lawrence had to offer, she was sure she would never want to kiss another man. How could she? How could anyone else measure up?

Moaning, she took her hands and placed then on both sides of his face, holding him in an attempt to quell some of the passion. He wasn't having it. She knew he wouldn't stop until he was ready.

When he finally let up a little, resorting to soft teasing pecks, she groaned. His kiss had blindsided her and she had no clue how to recuperate from the seductive assault. She had no idea how she was going to deal with her overwhelming desire for a man who didn't believe a word she said and who thought she was a criminal.

* * *

Lawrence eased up, stood and reached out his hand. She took it and he helped her up from the ground.

He had no idea what had possessed him to kiss her. He only knew that when he looked at her standing there—so sweet, innocent and passionate about wanting to work with at-risk youth—something inside of him melted. He wanted to wrap her in his arms, love her and keep her safe.

Yes, he was developing feelings for Minerva Jones. And when he really thought about all of his out-of-character actions as far as she was concerned, he realized that he had felt something for her from the first moment he saw her.

Where did that leave him when he wasn't even sure if she were a criminal or not?

"We should probably walk back to the house now."

She nibbled her lower lip and nodded, her face flushed and her eyes filled with passion. It was all he could do not to kiss her again. He reached over and brushed a leaf off her shoulder, grazing her cheek lightly. He felt a tingle shoot from his hand to his chest.

As they headed back to the house in silence, he couldn't believe he had almost made love to her—outside in broad daylight. He'd been that close, that senselessly aroused, that open. Was she indeed on the up-and-up? For all he knew she could have been the ringleader behind her brother and the McKnights being murdered. Or maybe she really knew who did it and was lying about it. And if she could lie that well and have him setting aside all his normal reactions, then she was damn good, And damn dangerous.

He'd been burned before trusting the wrong person in the past, and a life had been lost.

He wasn't trying to go that way again.

When they entered the house, she hadn't said a word and he had been deep in thought. She went into the study and picked up the book she'd been reading before they left.

"Who killed your brother and the McKnights, Minerva?" He knew he had a hard edge to his voice, but he couldn't help it.

If she were trying to play him…

She looked up at him and squinted. "Maybe you should just take me back to Paterson and let them kill me, too, Lawrence. Because I can't continue to try and prove to you that I'm telling the truth. I don't know."

"Okay, what made you leave Los Angeles and come to Jersey? Had you been keeping in that close of contact with the McKnights? Why? Something is missing."

"They were very close friends of my brother. I didn't have anywhere else to go."

"So your brother didn't have any friends in Los Angeles? You had to come all the way to Jersey? You didn't have any friends? No one from school? I just find it hard to believe that your brother is murdered and the first thing you think to do is run."

She blinked and paused.

He narrowed his eyes.

She's holding back something. I can't trust her.

She nodded. "I'm done. Done." She got up and calmly walked out of the room. It was all he could do not to follow her.

"You'd like me to slam the door, jerk. I know you would. But I have home training. I was raised right, and I'm not going to give you the satisfaction," she mumbled to herself and she carefully shut the door to her bedroom. She wasn't going to storm through the beautiful house as if she had no class, no matter how angry the detective made her.

How could someone as well trained as he was get it all so wrong?

She buried her head in her pillow and screamed.

She started to tell him that David was in Los Angeles and he was the one who told her to leave. But she didn't want to drag David even further into her brother's mess. David had a nice, honest life. As a businessman at a top firm, he had worked hard to make it out of South Central. He had tried to help Calvin and he had helped her more than enough. She wouldn't name him to anyone if she could help it, not even her dashing detective.

And how did they go from making out hot and heavy under the trees all the way back to his interrogation mode?

For the first time she felt like she was really ready to go all the way with a guy. She didn't have the stress of school and a job that made relationships and getting to know men difficult. And she didn't have her overprotective, gang-banger and *all-the-time-blocking* brother there to scare the guy away. And who does she develop an attraction to? *A cop.*

Maybe it was for the best. She had waited this long to lose her virginity; she might as well wait until she met a man who at *least* trusted her.

Frustration didn't even begin to describe her feelings. His kisses and caresses had unleashed something inside her. Against all her better judgment, she wanted to be with him. She knew she wouldn't be able to resist her desire. She just hoped she wouldn't regret it.

Chapter 9

When she hadn't come back downstairs, Lawrence decided to do some thinking about the case, trying to figure out what she was keeping from him. The more he thought about it, the less likely it seemed that she really was a criminal mastermind.

But she *was* hiding something.

It wasn't until she'd come into the study to tell him that dinner was done that he realized he'd spent the entire day mulling over and hashing out all the angles, yet he still wasn't anywhere near figuring her out.

And the fact she had once again prepared a meal that knocked his socks off left him even more confused. *She can cook like my mother!* He didn't take any pleasure in the fact that his long-standing line to keep him forever single was coming back to bite him in the behind. How did a woman her age learn to cook like that? It was just one of the many contradictions surrounding Minerva Jones.

He got up to clean the kitchen. He hadn't said much during dinner except to tell her the food was delicious. She accepted the compliment gracefully. But it was clear she could do without conversation. Or at least she could do without talking to him.

"I'll help," she said.

"That's okay. You cooked. You don't have to clean up, too."

"I don't mind. You wash and I'll dry. And tomorrow you're cooking for me, Detective." She nudged him playfully and he could tell it was her way of trying to call a truce.

Damn if he didn't want to take her peace offering.

He smiled. "Okay, Minerva. I'll make you the best breakfast you've ever tasted, and the best turkey and cheese sandwiches for lunch."

"*Whatever.* Get to washing."

They cleaned up in silence and perfect harmony. It felt comfortable and right. And he was determined to keep the warm feelings between them, to spark them up even more. Just when she turned to leave the kitchen, he pulled her into his arms.

Feeling her petite curvy body in his arms pushed all thoughts of suds and ages to the side. Thoughts of how right she felt underneath him when they were making out on the bed of leaves, how he'd come so close to making love to her, and how her mouth tasted like the sweetest candy he had ever savored, pushed past any common sense he had. The only thing he could think of was to finish what they had started earlier.

He allowed his lips to plunder and peruse. She opened to him automatically and her tongue met his with matching passion and desire. As he suckled on her soft lips, he couldn't help but roam her body. Her delicate curves had his mind spinning. Before he knew it, he had picked her up and carried her into the nearest bedroom. As he fell back on the bed, he pulled her on top of him and continued to caress her lips with his own.

He would never get tired of kissing her. Her groans hinted that she might feel a fraction of the same thing he was feeling. He let his hands lift her shirt. He massaged her breasts and felt the soft smooth silkiness of her skin.

He wanted her. He had to have her.

Now.

He halted the kiss and started to remove her shirt so that he could feast on her perfect breasts. Her eyes widened for a moment, but then she held up her arms so that he could take away the annoying barrier. He threw the shirt to the floor and quickly did the same with her bra.

"Lovely." He sat up and covered one nipple with his mouth as he massaged the other with his hands.

"Mmm." Her head went back and she moaned, "Lawrence." His name came out in a pant.

He sucked harder and began a soft twist and twirl of the other nipple with his thumb and forefinger.

"Ahhh… Ahhh… Lawrence."

He could get used to the way she said his name. Her body started to shake and that only made him up the ante. He let his hand slide down to her jeans and unbuttoned them. He positioned her so she was now lying on the bed and he slid her pants off. He decided to leave the lacy underwear on for now and just slide them to the side as he began to probe her heated sex with his fingers.

God, she was tight, so tight. He stroked her folds and her pleasure spot as his mouth found her nipple again. When she cried out in ecstasy, he knew she was ready. And he was more than ready. He stood and removed his pants, taking the protection out of his pocket and removing it with all the fervor he felt. He slid the lacy panties off her and positioned himself between her legs.

As he moved to enter her, he found her wet but almost impenetrably tight. He didn't want to hurt her. So he slowly eased back and forth small inches at a time. He placed his hand between them, touching her pleasure spot and coaxing her to open for him. Soon she was moving her hips tentatively. He took that as a sign to move completely into her and thrust forward as gently as he could. He wasn't prepared for the resistance he met until it was too late.

It had been feeling so good, so incredibly good, so unlike anything she had ever experienced. The initial sting of him entering her completely gave her a moment of pause. It caused her to close her eyes as she tried to get used to the sudden fullness.

He had stopped moving altogether and she was afraid to look at him.

"Open your eyes, Minerva," he demanded in a barely controlled voice.

She had never been this close to anyone, ever. Slowly the stinging ebbed away and in its place remained heightened sensations of desire. She arched her back and moved her hips.

"Don't move. Be still. I don't want to hurt you. Ahhhhhh… You should have told me."

"I'm sorry, Lawrence. I'm…I'm okay…honest. Please don't stop."

He let out a hiss of breath and for a minute she thought he was going to get up and walk away.

"We should stop," he said, his voice strained.

She opened her eyes and moved her hips again. But she had no idea how to move them in a way to get him to continue, to finish what he started. She hadn't really felt anything since her brother's murder and she needed to feel. She needed this. She needed him.

"Please, Lawrence, show me how. Show me what to do."

His stony, determined stare changed and he covered her mouth with a soul-stealing kiss just as he began to move his hips slowly, in and out. He rocked her, lulling her with the comfort of his loving.

This was it. This was what she knew would happen the very first time she set eyes on him. She predicted he would be her undoing. And sure enough, every one of her nerve endings had begun to unravel and shock her into the ultimate pleasure. She had never really known what she'd been missing.

He broke off his kiss and started to move his hips faster and faster.

"Minerva…oh, baby…"

Her sex tightened and she exploded as she moved to meet him thrust for thrust. His arm wrapped around her body embracing her and resting at her buttocks. He pulled her body so close to his she could hardly tell where she ended and where he began.

"Ahhhh…" She moaned.

"Scream, darling. Let it out, baby."

She did. She hollered loud and long as her orgasm raced through her.

He wasn't far behind her and soon he was screaming out her name.

He pulled out and she felt an enormous amount of wetness. When she heard him curse she looked up.

"The stupid condom broke. Damn!"

Uh-oh. That's not good.

She nibbled on her lips in contemplation. What were the odds the first time she decided to make love with a man the condom would break? Given the fact she was on the run and shouldn't have been having sex with a cop anyway, the odds were probably very high.

And the way Lawrence paced the room naked, wearing only his brooding glare and mumbling, let her know any romantic mood they could have had in the aftermath had been ruined by the shattered prophylactic.

What the heck is he all hot and bothered about? He's the one who's done this before and could be disease-ridden.

It was damn near insulting and she never took well to being insulted.

"I don't have anything, you know. So you can calm down with the pacing and cursing," she snapped at him and tried to push back the hurt feelings welling up in her chest.

He stared at her for a moment. "I don't have anything, either, if that's what you're implying. And disease isn't the only thing to worry about. I'm assuming that since you were a virgin you weren't on birth control?"

So much for holding the hurt feelings at bay…

He was worried that he might have gotten her pregnant as if, God forbid, he were to have a child with the likes of her. How she wished she could burst his bubble and proclaim that she was protected. But she wasn't on the Pill or any other form of birth control.

Getting up slowly, she reached for her clothes and started to get dressed. Once dressed, she moved to leave the room. He took her arm, halting her.

"Are you on the Pill or anything, Minerva?"

She could only shake her head, her voice totally lost to the mess she had made of everything. But she vowed that she would find the voice to cuss him out if he had a fit because she wasn't on birth control. She didn't know she was going to move to New Jersey, be shot at, fall in love with a cop and give up her virginity to him in a gorgeous house in the Poconos. How did she know she would need to be on the Pill? And did she really just admit that she was in love with him?

She wasn't ready to admit that, not even to herself. So that thought could just move on back to the far reaches of her conscious mind, where it belonged.

He wrapped his arms around her. Pulling her close, he planted a tender kiss on her forehead. "I'm sorry, baby. I should have protected you better. I'll do better next time."

Her face twisted in confusion. He wasn't mad at her? He blamed himself?

What. The. Hell?

"It wasn't your fault the condom broke, Lawrence. It wasn't anyone's fault. But can we change the subject? Better yet, can I just leave this incredibly embarrassing situation altogether and go hang my head in shame alone."

He stood back and seemed to notice for the first time that she was fully clothed. "You could do that. Or…you could take those clothes off and join me in the hot tub. I'm sure you must be pretty sore right about now. The hot tub would be good for you. Let me take care of you, Minerva."

He squinted, studying her every expression. And she was sure her face was a sight to see. She had never felt so confused in her life.

He pulled on his jeans and took her hand.

"Come on. A nice soak in the hot tub will do you good. And I promise to be on my best behavior." The sexy gleam in his eyes suggested anything but.

Yet she followed him, anyway.

She had never been in a hot tub before. But she had to admit he was right. The aching soreness that had taken over her body after their lovemaking slowly ebbed away. And, luckily, for the first fifteen minutes or so, Lawrence was content just holding her and not talking about the embarrassing, but oh-so-satisfying chain of events that had led them there.

"So what made you wait until you were twenty-six years old to have sex? And why me?"

It couldn't last for long…

She had just gotten comfortable and was working on putting the incident behind her.

"Try having a social life with a gang-banging brother always getting in your business. He scared away all the nice and not-so-nice guys alike. After a while, I decided to just focus on school and work, getting my degree. And I figured when the right guy came along, Calvin wouldn't be able to intimidate him or scare him away. He'd be the one…"

He cleared his throat and his voice came out kind of strained. "So why me, Minerva?"

You. Are. So-oo. The. One.

But she wasn't even about to go there. She was hardly ready. And based on the strain in his voice and the apprehensive expression on his face, neither was he.

"No worries, Detective Hightower. I'm not pegging

you for the love of my life…" *Liar. Liar. Liar.* The words blazed in her mind like an alarm going berserk. "I just figured since we're both so attracted to each other, and there's not much else for us to do while we're hiding out here. We might as well explore our attraction."

Her words sounded so bold and brazen. She leaned over and placed her lips on his. She nipped his bottom lip with her teeth and nibbled seductively. She trailed the kisses to his neck and chest.

He inhaled deeply as if trying to control himself. "Watch out there, baby. You're still sore. I can't promise I'd be able to restrain myself if you got me started again. I will ride you hard and put you through your paces. You'd be soaking for days to get rid of that sweet ache."

Dang! Good. God!

She stopped her kissing and stared at him. A devilish grin crossed his face. She assumed he must have thought he'd scared her off. She wished she had a camera for the shocked expression on his face when she straddled his lap and kissed him full on the lips with everything inside her. He didn't need much coaxing at all. He opened his mouth and plundered hers, taking over the kiss with very little effort. His hand trailed her body in the water. All she could feel was silky wetness and strong touches, focused touches, marking touches. Every spot he caressed he owned.

"Lawrence…" she moaned when his hand moved to her core and stroked her there. She writhed on his lap wildly as an orgasm ripped through her at the first swipe of his skilled fingers across her slick folds.

"You were warned, baby. You didn't listen. I told you about being hardheaded and stubborn. Now you have to learn your lesson. It's a hard lesson to learn. But by the morning you might get the hang of it." He grinned that sexy grin of his as he reached for his jeans, resting next to the hot tub, and pulled the protection from his pocket. He moved her long enough to sheath himself first with the condom and then in her, deep and all-encompassing.

"Ohhh…" It felt glorious with steamy water all around them. She started to move her hips, rocking back and forth and moving up and down, her knees bracing her on either side of his strong muscular thighs.

"Yes. Mmm…baby…yes." His hands grabbed her hips, halting her movement.

Perplexed, she stared at him. "What's wrong?"

"I got this, baby. Time for your first lesson." He lifted her slowly and slid her back down his slick soulful shaft.

She groaned. It felt so good, so achingly good.

He kept at it, moving her up and down, slowly, over and over again and again until she thought she would get seasick. The sound of the water splashing and the feel of her own wetness overwhelmed her. She felt soaked, but she knew one feeling was just out of her reach and it would remain out of her reach as long as he controlled her movements the way he was.

"Lawrence…please…"

He smiled. She covered his mouth in a passionate kiss and he held her suspended with just the tip of his sex resting inside of her. She twirled her tongue and nibbled his lips earnestly.

"Please, Lawrence…"

He groaned and picked up his pace, moving her up and down harder and faster, touching spots inside her she had never known existed and sending off rockets in her core.

She screamed and screamed again. She loved the feel of her breasts bouncing fast, up and down, up and down. She wrapped her arms around him on the down-stroke and clung to him the way her sex pulsed and tightened around his. A soft sigh escaped her lips and she shook.

He laughed and lifted her off his lap, positioning her so that she was kneeling on the bench of the hot tub and her hands grasping the edge. He entered her again from behind, stroking in sure possessive measures. He moved in and out with such powerful quickness she would have started speaking in tongues if she knew how. She moved her hips in circles, meeting his every thrust. All she could do was mumble and sigh and moan and grunt, at least until she had to scream. Then she turned around to look at him.

His scream followed hers as he grabbed her and held her close to him, his sex still pulsing hotly inside her. They remained like that for a couple of minutes, each panting in satisfaction. The warm water felt so good and he felt even better.

* * *

She smiled and stretched as she yawned and remembered all the ways that Lawrence had taught her lessons, *all night lon*g. He hadn't been making idle threats. They were really hard lessons. It was a good thing she was such a quick study.

She sat up just in time to see Lawrence come into the room with a tray full of food. There was coffee, fruit and French toast—enough for an army. He probably hadn't eaten himself yet. She figured the bulk of the food had to be for him.

"Aww…did you cook all this for lil' ol' me?"

"I told you I had you for breakfast and lunch… And if you're really good, I might just throw some steaks on the grill for dinner and some baked potatoes in the oven. And I make a mean hot fudge sundae."

"Well, now, just exactly how good does a girl have to be? And can't I be a little bad?" She stretched her arms and arched her back as she winked at him.

His gaze heated up to a sensual simmer. "You need to eat and get your strength up, baby. I can see you're ready for another lesson or two." He cut the French toast with a fork, dipped it in the syrup and fed it to her.

"Umm…full service. A girl could get used to this."

She picked up one of the strawberries, dunked it in the bowl of whipped cream and placed it near his mouth. He opened his mouth for a taste and she placed it in her own mouth instead, making a show of chewing.

He smiled a devilish smile as he watched her. "Oh, yes, baby, eat up and eat well, you're going to need your strength for sure."

Chapter 10

He was getting in too deep and the only problem was he didn't want to get out. If Minerva Jones wasn't the perfect woman for him, then the perfect woman for him, didn't exist.

He flipped the steaks on the grill, happy for the slight chill in the air. He hated grilling in the summer, but liked to crank up the fire in the fall and winter. When the patio door opened he turned to see that Minerva had woken up from her nap and joined him.

They had spent most of the day in bed. And if he hadn't worked up such an appetite, he might have been content to just lie there holding her until she got her energy back.

He couldn't contain his grin at the sight of her. "Look who's finally awake."

"Yeah, you went to sleep first. So it's only fitting that I woke up later. I had to listen to your snoring before I could doze off." She smirked as she took a seat on the teak lounge chair.

"Well, at least my snoring didn't wake you up out of a dead sleep," he teased. Her snoring didn't really wake him up. She actually had a cute little half wheeze, half-breathe snore.

"I don't snore…that bad…" She giggled and leaned back on the lounge. "The steaks smell great. I'm starved."

"Worked up an appetite, huh?" He flipped the steaks and closed the grill before giving her his full attention.

"Yes, I did. I think I've learned my lesson." She shot him a sly glance and licked her lips.

He gave her a mock stern stare. "I'll be the judge of that, baby. I think you need a little more schooling."

She laughed. "It's really nice up here. The air smells so crisp, so fresh. It feels like a world away from Paterson and definitely a world away from smog-filled Los Angeles."

He took a gulp of air. The refreshing mountain air was a big change from Jersey. He'd forgotten how nice it was to just come up here when it's not ski season.

"Do you miss home?"

"Sometimes. I miss my brother the most. And I miss…some friends. But I think I would be really lonely if I were in Los Angeles now. I miss the social worker—Valerie—who was always there for us. With Calvin gone, I don't have anyone else. The McKnights were the closest thing to family for me, and now they're gone."

The pause she gave troubled him. Who did she miss in Los Angeles? A boyfriend? Maybe the person who was after her? He suddenly had an overwhelming need to get the truth out of her again.

"And don't you want their deaths vindicated?"

"Of course!"

"Then why aren't you helping the police? Why didn't you stay and talk with the LAPD? Why aren't you doing everything you can to help us find the people who killed the McKnights?"

Her beautiful eyes formed big circles and she looked as if she'd been struck. She squinted and then stood. The hurt expression on her face cut him deeper than if he had hurt himself.

Yes, he was in too deep. That's why he had to make sure that she was on the up-and-up. He had trusted in the past and been burned. He didn't know if he could take it if Minerva proved to be lying to him.

"I'll go make a salad and check on your baked potatoes." She didn't wait for his response. She didn't tell him to kiss her behind, *nothing*. She just left him standing there at the grill.

If he could have taken the hurt out of her eyes, he would have. But he needed to know what he was dealing with. He didn't feel like getting caught on the bad end of a surprise.

Not again. Not *ever* again.

He placed the steaks on a plate and covered them

with foil to rest before they ate. Once inside the house, he found her in the kitchen.

She had the salad fixings out and she was pouring olive oil into a bowl as she whisked it with the rest of her dressing ingredients.

He didn't say anything. He just watched her chop and dice and then pour what appeared to be some kind of homemade dressing onto the salad.

They ate in silence for a little while and then she cleared her throat.

"I think that we should probably stop this…this… whatever we're doing. It seemed like a good idea at the time but in hindsight it really wasn't. You don't trust me and I don't blame you. But I can't continue to be this open and share this much of myself and still have you treating me like an immoral liar. If I knew who killed my brother or Tommy or Timmy, I would tell you. I would have told the police. If I had gone to the LAPD, it would have been a waste. I had nothing to tell them. But it only took me leaving the police department in Paterson to get shot at."

His gut clenched. This wasn't what he wanted. He wanted her to be open with him and tell him what she was holding back. He didn't want her to break off what they had started to share. He cleared his throat. "So you want to end this?"

"I don't want to. I *have* to. For my own good… You're…" Her lower lip trembled and he felt a sharp pain in his heart.

He had to try and make her see where he was coming from.

"When I was sixteen, I used to run with a pretty bad crowd. We thought we were too cool for school, work, anything that even hinted at respectable. We cut classes so much that a few of the guys in the crew even ended up getting kicked out of Eastside High School during the days of Joe Clark. I had always kept up with my schoolwork, at least enough to pull Cs and Ds. So I didn't get kicked out. I had a cousin who was the same age as me, Michael, the chief's baby brother. Anyway, we had been tight growing up. But once I got with that crew, I didn't want Mike around ruining my rep. He always found a way to tag along, though.

"We were all cutting school and hanging out. The most we had ever done before was drink liquor we could steal from our parents' cabinets or that we could pay an old drunk to buy for us. But on this day, Johnny decided to bring drugs. I didn't know there were drugs there. I never would have suspected my friends of having anything to do with drugs. And while my cousin was a nuisance and I didn't want him hanging around, I believed with all my heart that he was safe there. But he wasn't."

He took a deep breath. He had never really talked to anyone but his father about how he really felt, how guilty he felt. And that had been years ago, when it happened. He tried not to talk about it a lot, opting instead to just live his life in a way that would honor Michael's memory. But if talking about it would get Minerva to understand where he was coming from and trust him, so that he could trust her, he had to open up.

Taking another deep breath and running his hand across his head, he continued. "A bunch of them got high in the basement and then thought it would be cool to play Russian roulette with a handgun. My cousin died high on weed in a basement all because I trusted the wrong people, including a girl I loved who was part of the crew.

"My family forgave me and said that it wasn't my fault. I didn't make him take the drugs or hold the gun to his head. But I don't believe that. He was a good person. He wanted to continue the Hightower legacy of public service and be a cop one day. And now he'll never be able to.

"You're holding something back, Minerva, I can tell. And, I won't be able to trust you until you trust me enough to tell me what it is."

She couldn't help but stare at him. She had told him everything she knew. The only thing she had left out was David's involvement in helping her get out of town. But bringing David further into this mess was *not* an option.

"Then I guess it's really best that we end things now, Lawrence. I've told you everything I know. And while I can see where your distrust is coming from, it hurts too much to keep doing this. I *can't* continue to do this." Her entire heart was on the line. Couldn't he tell?

He nodded. "So that's it?"

"Yeah. Maybe once the murderers are caught and you realize that I'm not a criminal. Maybe then we can see."

She wanted to tell him that she loved him. That she

trusted him with her life. She wanted to, but she knew she couldn't. He probably wouldn't believe her anyway.

She got up and started clearing the table. "I'll clean up tonight, since you cooked."

He shook his head. "I'll help."

As much as she wanted to tell him that she just wanted to be alone with her thoughts, she recognized the hard glint in his eyes. He was going to stay and help because that's what he wanted to do.

At least he had the decency not to talk. Or maybe he had an attitude and was just withholding speech. Whatever the reason for the silence, she welcomed it.

When they were done, he ran his hand across his head. "It's early still, Minerva. Do you want to watch a movie or something? We have a pretty decent collection of DVDs here."

She shook her head, even though it would have made her so happy to spend the evening wrapped in his arms, laughing and enjoying a film, maybe even having some popcorn. It sounded positively divine. She wished she could have said yes.

But now that she realized how much she felt for him— how deeply his distrust had the potential to hurt her— she had to protect herself. She had to protect her heart.

"No, I'm thinking I'll just turn in early and read that Toni Morrison novel until I doze off. I'll see you in the morning."

"Minerva…" His voice trailed off and she knew it was because he couldn't say what she wanted to hear.

He really couldn't trust her and if he couldn't trust her she knew she couldn't continue to make love to him.

Since his conversation with Minerva didn't go anywhere near where he wanted it to, Lawrence decided to just watch a film by himself and figure out another way to get at what she was keeping from him.

His feelings for her wouldn't allow him to just pretend he didn't want the truth. And they damn sure wouldn't let him stop pressing her for honesty. He had to admit he hadn't expected her to just cut him off and halt their exploration. That threw him for a loop. It had him almost questioning if he could just let it slide.

Almost.

The buzz of his cell phone pulled him from his thoughts and he saw that it was Kendall calling.

"What's up, Chief?"

"We picked up the folks in the white van. They had the same guns they'd used to shoot at you and Ms. Jones on them. The forensics just came back. None of their guns were the guns that killed the McKnights, however. We're trying to get them to talk. But so far all they're saying is they were working for someone who wanted them to get the girl."

His blood chilled. "A hit?"

"No, they claim they were just supposed to grab her."

"Yeah, so why were they shooting at her?" He let out a hiss of air. The thought of Minerva in danger had an unnerving effect on him. He didn't like it one bit.

"They won't say. It's gonna be tough to get them to

talk. Whoever they're working for must be a really scary character. These guys look pretty hard-core and they're facing hard time. But so far they won't talk."

He gritted his teeth, imagining all the ways he could make them talk. "Oh, I'll bet I could make them talk. I'm coming back up there."

"Hold off on that for a minute, Lawrence. Let's see what else we can turn up here. Until we know who hired these guys, she's still in danger. How is she, by the way?"

He paused, taking his mind off the criminals for a moment. There was something about the sound of Kendall's voice that made him uneasy. "What do you mean by that?"

"What do you mean, what do I mean? How is she? Is she talking yet? You two called a truce? I'm assuming since I'm talking to you and you sound fine, you two haven't done each other bodily harm."

"Yeah. We're good. She's fine."

"Mmm-hmm… Interesting." There it was again, that weird, all-knowing, putting-two-and-two-together-and-getting-a-million tone in Kendall's voice that made him stop and wonder what his cousin thought he knew.

"What?" He had a feeling he would regret asking Kendall that question.

"You forget, I've known you since you were a snot-nosed kid, you and your brothers running around the house with Michael. I can tell when something's up with you. You like her, don't you?"

Hearing Kendall mention Michael's name when he had just opened up to Minerva about his guilt about his cousin's death brought everything full circle. He couldn't give up on getting her to tell him everything. He couldn't risk it.

"It doesn't matter, Kendall. It's not going to stop me from doing my job if she turns out to be dirty." He leaned his head back on the chair and willed the conversation over.

"I don't think she's dirty, Lawrence. I'm just worried that whoever her brother crossed in Los Angeles will end up getting to her before we can get them, or the LAPD can get them. I'm waiting to hear back from the detective in the LAPD who's been looking into the murder. Victor Morales. We've been playing phone tag." Kendall paused. "My gut tells me she's scared. She's holding something back. But she's not a criminal."

"Well, she still won't talk. She still won't say who killed her brother or who's after her." Uneasy about the neediness he heard in his own voice he tried to push it from his thoughts. There was really no way around it. He realized that he needed her to open up to him.

"Maybe she really doesn't know."

"You said it yourself, she's holding something back... Did you say Victor Morales? I think that's Maritza's brother...Penny's friend."

"Really? I didn't know that. If I ever get him on the phone, I'll ask him. As for Ms. Jones, maybe we're asking the wrong questions. Let us put the squeeze on these two white van idiots and then maybe we'll have more to go on with her."

Lawrence gritted his teeth. Waiting around for

someone else to do the investigating and find the information went against his nature. He ran his hand across his head in frustration and let out a hiss of breath.

"We're on it, here. I'll call you in a couple of days—"

"A couple of days!"

"You're the one who wanted to take some personal time. You all but volunteered to watch out for Ms. Jones. What, are you getting cabin fever now? Can't hang?" Kendall had the nerve to chuckle.

"Just call me as soon as you find something. And we might want to look into another safe house for Minerva. Because if you guys don't find out who's after her soon, I'm coming back."

"So, it's Minerva now…hmm."

"That is her name."

"Mmm-hmm… All right, Lawrence. I'll be in touch as soon as we know more."

Lawrence hung up his cell phone and shook his head. He must really have it bad if his cousin could tell there was something going on between him and Minerva over the phone. He hoped he could contain whatever he was starting to feel for her until he was sure she wasn't a crook. And he most definitely hoped it wasn't too late to put a halt to his emotions.

Even as he thought that he had to laugh. He was about half-past too late.

The soft knock on the door caused her to look up from her book. She really hoped Lawrence wasn't going to try to tempt her with his delicious and *oh-so-fine* body, because she wouldn't be able to resist.

Be strong! Resist temptation. "Come in."

He opened the door and walked into her room. "Are you sure you don't want to watch a movie, play some cards, checkers, chess, dominoes, anything? I'm bored." He gave her the perfect set of pleading puppy-dog eyes.

She smiled. The man probably never had any problems getting exactly what he wanted from women. Who could say no to that face, that strong, determined, handsome face? He had that good man/bad boy thing going on full blast, like her favorite actor, Idris Elba. Hell, he even looked like the actor.

She put the book down and stood. "I should warn you… If we play any of those games…I'm going to wipe the floor with you. I'm going to pretty much annihilate you in any game you pick. So if you're one of those men whose ego is bruised easily when beaten by a woman, you should run along." She made sweeping movements with her hands.

He grinned his sexy grin and his eyes gleamed. He was daring her. "Oh, you're just going to start talking smack early, huh? It's going to be fun to beat you at something. Hell, I'll even be a gentleman and let you choose the game."

"Okay, but you're going to regret that, Detective."

"Do not pass, go. Go directly to jail."

He regretted it all right.

Lawrence stewed with a partial grin on his face. She

had beaten him at just about every game in the house. And she was now proving to be a real estate mogul to boot by wiping the floor with him in Monopoly.

"And don't think I've forgotten that you still owe me money for squatting on my property. I'm gonna need you to pay up, brother man." She offered with a grin as she put up more hotels, apartments and businesses on the board.

"You must be cheating at these games somehow," he grumbled.

"See there. I warned you ahead of time, but you didn't listen. Don't hate the player, hate the game or, in your case, games…" She burst out laughing before breaking out into a yawn. "I'm getting kinda tired. Why don't we just call this one and say I beat you yet again."

"No one likes a sore winner… And we haven't played every game in the house yet. I have to beat you at something." He got up and looked through the closet where they kept all the games and decks of cards.

The only thing left was the Karaoke machine. He grinned as he thanked God for the time he'd spent in the youth choir at Mt. Zion and the fact that he could actually carry a tune. He'd bet little miss game maverick couldn't sing.

He pulled out the machine and brought it into the den. She was putting away the Monopoly pieces and stopped to stare at him.

"Trust me, you don't want to get into it with me, De-tective." She laughed. "Look, I'm sleepy. I couldn't *possibly* beat you at anything else. Plus, Karaoke is no fun with two people and it's really only fun when people can't sing." She put her hands on her hips for effect, and he wondered how he was going to get through the rest of the night not being able to touch those delectable hips of hers.

"And how would we make it a competition, anyway?" She asked.

"Good question. I got it. We each pick the songs for the other and the first person to cave and not sing the song is the loser."

She nodded. "I'm telling you now..."

"Yeah, yeah, I'll be sorry... You're gonna beat me... blah, blah, blah." He got started looking for a song that she would refuse so he could go to bed having beaten her at least once. It would be a small victory, but a victory nonetheless.

"Hmm, someone sounds like a sore loser. Well, since you want to be so snippy, losers go first. I'll have a song for you in a moment." She busied herself looking through the special Karaoke CDs and he did the same.

"Found yours." The smile on her face gave him pause as he looked at the song she was pointing at on the CD.

"'Achy Breaky Heart'? You've got to be kidding. Why do we even have anything by Billy Ray Cyrus in here? This must have come with the machine." He frowned. He didn't want to sing the song.

"You could always forfeit. You made the rules. If you don't want to sing it, we can just keep my little winning streak going." She grinned and leaned back on the sofa.

No way! He riffled through the CDs and grinned. "Found yours, too. You can mull it over while I perform my show-stopping rendition of 'Achy Breaky Heart.'"

She looked at the song he'd picked for her. Her eyes narrowed and her lips pursed.

There was no way his little hip-hop feminist would perform that song. He had this one in the bag.

He sang the country music song. He even did a quick and dirty version of what he thought a country line dance might be, well, a country version of the cha-cha slide anyway.

When he finished she clapped. "Look at you, carrying a tune and getting your little two-step on. I ain't mad at ya. But you're about to go down. I know you thought I would rather forfeit than sing this little song you picked for me. But I don't cave. I take no pris-oners and I play to win. Since you did a little dance with yours, I think I'll even treat you to a dance. Good thing this is a cordless mic."

He swallowed. Something told him he was in trouble.

Her seductive dance moves didn't have anything on her voice. She sang like an angel.

Mesmerized, he stared at her with his mouth open and his eyes hooded. By the time she straddled him at the end of the song and finished it off in a soft, sexy pant, he was done.

She gazed into his eyes for a few minutes before standing up. "I was going to warn you before I was rudely interrupted. My mother was an awesome singer and my dad was a very talented musician before he got hooked on heroin. Music is in my blood, even though I would never make a career out of it. *Still* wanna play Karaoke?"

He shook his head and tried to compose himself after that sensuous song that ended in a seductive lap dance. "No. You win. You're the best."

He got up and hugged her before planting his lips on hers. She kissed him back with pent-up passion for a full minute before pulling away.

"I was serious, Lawrence. We can't do this. I can't. I'm sorry." She backed away before turning and leaving.

He sat back down on the sofa. Contemplating the many ways Minerva Athena Jones was proving him wrong about everything he thought about her. She certainly lived up to her names, though. The *virgin goddess of the more disciplined side of war, cunning intelligence and the inventor of music, indeed.* She had certainly used the gift of song to wipe him out in battle! He smiled. It was going to be fun figuring her out.

Chapter 11

After a full day of being politely cordial with one another and trying to act as if they hadn't shared the most body-rocking, mind-altering chemistry either of them had ever experienced, Lawrence was pretty sure he was going to lose it. He hadn't gotten any sleep after their night of games because he kept thinking about what it had felt like to have her in his arms as they'd both drifted off to sleep. That was how they should have ended last night, not in separate beds.

He wanted her back in his arms again.

"I want to trust you, Minerva." He realized that he really did, more than he could convey. He suddenly felt as if his future happiness was riding on his being able to trust her. And he wanted to be happy.

He remembered the silly toast that he and his brothers had made the same night he had approached Minerva in the bar. He and his brothers had toasted to happiness. If he were prone to have even the slightest sense of humor, he would have found the entire situation funny.

She took a sip of her coffee and stared at him. "I'm sure you do want to trust me. But you can't and it's cool. We can't always have what we want."

That's where she was so wrong. He wanted her and he fully intended to have her. She was just going to have to learn to open up and trust him.

"Look, Minerva, I might not be the most patient guy in the world. But I know that some things are worth waiting for. As long as we can wait it out together, I'm willing to work on building the trust between us. I know you don't fully trust me either, do you?"

She blinked. "Does it matter?"

"Hell, yes, it matters. Are you going to sit there and pretend that it doesn't? Are you going to tell me that I'm the only one feeling what's going on between us?"

She stared at him for a moment, her gaze hesitant and somber. "Why are you doing this?"

"Because I need you, Minerva. I need you to trust me. I need to trust you. I just need you."

"You just want to have sex. I know I said we could have an affair while we're here, but it's getting too complicated. I—"

"You need me, too. And you're scared by how much you do." *So this is what it's like…begging?*

How did it come to this? How did Minerva Jones manage to slip into his heart and get him to the point where he was pleading for a chance?

She stood up to leave.

Oh, no, baby. No running. We are facing this today. Here and now, because I'm not going through another night without you in my arms. Hell, no.

He stood and walked over to her.

She tilted her head defiantly. She looked so cute, so sexy, so kissable. Those soft, pouty lips were just asking for him to plant one on her.

He took her face in his hands and let his fingers caress each of her lovely cheeks in his hold. He ran his thumb across her bottom lip first and then the top one. The touch was divine. Bending his head, he captured her mouth like the prize it was. She didn't resist. She opened her mouth and her tongue dashed in, licking his mouth with tantalizing strokes that would have driven him mad if he wasn't so determined to make her realize how deep he was falling, how important it was that she give them a chance.

Since he didn't need to hold her face in place, he let his hand slide down her back. Cupping her backside, he pulled her to him. She groaned and deepened her kiss.

He wanted to lift her and take her on the kitchen counter. It was all he could do to end the kiss and back away.

"No more running away from this, for either of us. I want to work on the trust. I want to be with you. I'm not letting you push me away."

She had her hand on her chest as if she were trying to catch her breath, but she looked up at his words. She slanted her left eye and twisted her lip. *"Letting me?"*

"That's right. When it comes to what is going on between us, I see that I'm going to have to be the one to call the shots, because I'm the only one willing to face what's happening. When you get a little less scared and stop trying to run, maybe we can share that responsibility."

She shook her head. "You're crazy, Lawrence."

He wanted to tell her that he was crazy about her, because he was. But he didn't. Instead, he decided it was time to lay down the law, the law of desire.

"No more running from our feelings. No more not facing what's happening between us, and for damn sure, no more nights without you in my arms. We're going to work through this and face this together. We clear?"

She pursed her lips. He covered her mouth with his again, using his tongue, his lips and even his teeth to get her to see the light. As he nipped, nibbled, sucked, and feasted on her lusciousness, he couldn't help but acknowledge that he really could go on kissing her forever. He stopped only when he had gotten his fill.

Taking a deep breath he slanted his eye. "We clear, Minerva?"

"Crystal," she panted her response.

"Good. I'm going to do some work in the study. The sooner, we figure out who is trying to kill you, the sooner I can really focus all my attention on making you admit how much you need me, how much you need *us*."

He pulled her close and kissed her again, slowly, deliberately. Her tongue swirled and danced in his mouth. He picked up his pace joining her in their ever-growing passion. Her hands traveled up and down his chest and it made him curse the shirt he wore. He wanted those soft fingers on his skin. He groaned from deep in this gut. If he didn't want to take her right then and there in the kitchen, then he needed to stop.

Pulling away, he studied her as best as he could with his hooded gaze. The lust threatened to consume him whole as he took in her passion-blushed cheeks and kiss-swollen lips. Another feeling also bubbled up in him and it made him reach out and caress her face.

Gazing up at him with her big bright eyes, she purred sexily, "I think I'm going to like your methods, Detective." And then she giggled as she tried to wiggle away from his embrace. "I have to say that it might take a little more to convince me…"

He held her steady not wanting to let her go.

"You haven't seen anything yet. Us Hightower men can be very persuasive when it comes to getting the woman we want." And if that other feeling bubbling up in his heart was what he thought it was then "want" couldn't even begin to describe how important this woman was to him.

When her cell phone rang, she jumped. It hadn't rung in so long, she'd almost forgotten she had the thing. She'd attached the charger to the phone and kept it plugged into a socket in her bedroom. The only person who had called the phone David had given her was David, and she hadn't heard from him in a while.

She looked at the caller ID and saw that it was him.

"Hey, David."

"Where the hell are you?"

Taken aback by his nasty tone, she paused while her mouth literally gapped open.

"Where are you, Thena?" his words seemed to be compressed and coming from between clenched teeth. "Hello? I asked you a question."

"Timmy and Tommy were murdered and I had—"

"I know they were murdered. That's why I've been trying to find you. Where are you?"

"I'm fine. But the people who killed them haven't been caught. I'm safe and I'm trying to lay low. I don't want them to get me, too."

She heard him hiss. He sounded almost disgusted. *What the hell was wrong with him?*

"Look, I think whoever killed Timmy and Tommy and maybe even my brother might be the same people. They even tried to snatch me. Luckily, there was a cop there and he saved me…"

"Are you with the cop now? I told you to stay away from the cops. Do you want to get killed? Or do you want the folks who took out your brother and my cousins to take out this cop, too? How many people are you willing to get killed for you?" His voice sounded harsh and ugly to her ears, unlike anything she'd ever heard from him.

She shook her head. He was probably just upset about Timmy's and Tommy's deaths. They were his cousins, after all, and he might even blame himself and her a little for their deaths. If he hadn't sent her there, they would still be alive. The pang of guilt that had been threatening to overtake her since she walked into the apartment and found the twins murdered exploded in her chest and she bit back a gasp.

"I don't want anyone else to die. Including you, David. That's why I think it's best if I just stay away for a while…"

"Just tell me where the hell you are. I'll come and get you and we'll find someplace safe for you."

"I'm safe now. I'm good…" She thought she heard Lawrence in the hall and realized that if she was really going to repay David and keep him out of the mess her life had become, she'd better get off the phone. "I have to go, David. I'll be in touch when it's safe to do so. I'm really sorry about Timmy and Tommy. I'd just die if something happened to you, too—"

"And what about whoever you're with? Would you just *die* if something happened to him? Because the person you're messing with doesn't play. You need to tell me where you are before someone else ends up dead!" His voice sounded almost threatening and she figured he really must blame her for his cousins' deaths.

"I can't do that. I'm sorry. 'Bye." She hung up the phone and then turned off the ringer. David's tone of voice was ridiculous. Even if he was worried about her or blamed her, he had no business snapping at her like that. Willing to give him the benefit of the doubt, she also knew that she had been very close to telling him off.

Yes, it was best to just turn off the ringer.

A few days later Lawrence leaned back in the office chair and rubbed his head as he listened on the phone to Kendall relaying the latest from the home front. He wanted to be in the action. Even though he was having the most exhilarating time of his life getting to know Minerva, sitting in the Poconos, while his colleagues were trying to find out who killed the McKnights and who was after Minerva, went against every fiber of his being.

"So apparently the person who's after her is from California and he might have some ties with the drug cartel that is trying to set up shop in the Fourth Ward. The McKnights were supposed to be instrumental in that, but you shut that down when you sent them to jail five years ago. It looks like they weren't willing to play their positions when they got out of jail and that might have gotten them killed."

"So how does Minerva fit into this? Is she involved with drugs? The cartel?" She couldn't be involved with drugs. She just couldn't be.

"Still trying to figure that out. These clowns claim they don't know. They just know that the guy who paid them wanted her badly. Maybe it's a boyfriend? Lover?"

"Nah, he's not a lover." He only thought to halt his words after they had already fallen out of his mouth.

"How do you know?"

"He's not her lover. Leave it at that."

He could see Kendall shaking his head without even being in the same room with him. He could tell by the sigh and rueful chuckle coming across the phone lines.

"I don't even want to know. But I will say this… Be careful." Kendall paused. "Anyway…we're still working on these guys and asking questions around town. One name that came up when we spoke with LAPD about her brother's murder investigation and checked out the living relatives for the McKnights is David Sims. Apparently, he was the fourth member of their little crew and the four of them grew up together. He doesn't have a record but the LAPD has been watching him for a while. They just can't get anything to stick. Detective Morales just came across some evidence that allowed them to put a warrant out for his arrest. I still haven't spoken to Morales himself yet. He may be out looking for this Sims guy. But if the guy from California that hired the white van folks and Sims are the same person, then I definitely need to chat with Morales."

"David Sims, huh? I'll ask her about him."

"Yeah, you do that."

"Listen, I'm thinking I need to come and get involved with this investigation myself. We need to find a safe house for her."

"We can do that, Lawrence. Are you sure you would be cool with trusting her safety to others?"

Hell, no.

He paused. "Maybe we can hang out here for the rest of the week. But, y'all need to find out what's what with this one soon. I can't sit here doing nothing much longer."

"Soup's on…" A sweet voice beckoned to him from the doorway.

He looked up to find Minerva standing there looking sexy and waved her in. "I'll call you back later."

Kendall chuckled. "Yeah. You do that."

He hung up the phone and turned his attention to Minerva. Delightful smells had been wafting through the house, and he'd wondered what she had been up to in the kitchen.

"It smells great. What did you cook?"

"Spaghetti and meatballs."

"We had spaghetti sauce?"

"No. I used those tomatoes that were in the freezer and made some sauce from scratch. I hope that was okay…"

"It's fine, my mom has so many tomatoes from her garden that we all have them in our freezers and she stores some here and home. Trust me there are *plenty* more tomatoes left somewhere in a Hightower household. But look at you making not only pancakes from scratch, but sauce, too. Most women I know use that jar stuff."

Awed, he just stared at her.

She brushed a stray curl out of her eyes. "I'm not saying I won't use a jar, because I will. But if I have time and beautiful tomatoes like the ones from your mom's garden, I'm making my own. So come on. Let's eat before it gets cold."

"Come here first." He folded his arms across his chest and leaned against the desk.

She hesitated at first but then stepped into the room and walked over. "What's up? I know you don't want the food getting cold."

"Italian food always tastes good reheated." He pulled her into his arms and swooped down for a kiss.

She tasted like the most decadent dessert he'd ever savored. She gave new meaning to the phrase "give me some sugar." Her mouth epitomized confection sublime. Allowing his tongue to outline her lips and then sweep through her delectable mouth, he knew he would never get enough of kissing her. He wanted more.

Stopping the kiss went against every fiber of his being. But in order to do what he wanted to do, *no,* what he needed to do, he had to get those bothersome clothes off her. He made quick work of the offending objects and then spun her around so that she was leaning against the large mahogany desk where he had been only moments ago.

Bending his head, he feasted on her nipples first. He couldn't hold back his groans as he traveled farther down her body and ended up on his knees in front of her. He continued trailing kisses until his tongue reached her core. Then, he suckled and lapped in and all around her velvet folds. Time seemed to stand still and all he could hear was her labored breath. All he could feel was her shuddering pulse. It seemed to echo and vibrate all around him. Her soft pants and shaking thighs were the only things that gave a hint that he wasn't dreaming. He really was suckling on the greatest nectar known to man.

A moan escaped her lips and she squirmed. The pleasure must have been getting too intense for her, but he couldn't stop. He couldn't let her go. Soon she screamed loud and long. It could have been music if it wasn't so raw and filled with need. She wanted more. He could tell. He stood and turned her to face the desk. Pushing the papers and knickknacks onto the floor, he bent her over the desk.

"You're beautiful, Minerva."

She whimpered.

He didn't have time to get fully undressed himself. He needed to be in her. With mind-shattering quickness, he unzipped his pants, pulled out a condom and protected them before he tunneled deep inside her, not stopping until he reached the hilt.

Minerva cried out for what had to be the fifth or sixth time in a matter of minutes. How did he do it? How did he manage to make her body literally hum? His thrusts were powerful and all-consuming.

"I need you. I want you so bad, it might just drive me crazy."

"Mmm…" She couldn't talk in the midst of this. How was he able to talk? Didn't he feel the earth moving beneath them? Wasn't the emotion overload causing him to short-circuit? Was she the only one in the room who had to conserve enough energy to scream?

"I'm not going to be able to hold out much longer, baby. You feel so damn good." He moved his hips faster, as if that were possible, and he worked her like a strong, well-oiled piston.

"Does it feel good to you, baby? Let me know. I will stay here all night to please you."

"Mmm…mmm…mmm-hmm." Her grunts channeled into moans and gasps. Her nerve endings refused to lie dormant. Every inch of her body sizzled and popped with desire. She felt the waves of heat travel from the pit of her stomach to her core and tears trailed down her eyes.

She couldn't believe the man was making her feel so good it made her cry. Where was the rhyme or reason in that? Her heart thumped so loudly it rang in her ears. A sweet lump swelled in her chest and traveled to her throat. Emotions she didn't dare name overwhelmed her as she bit back a sob.

She loved him.

She had never been in love before, but she knew without a doubt that she loved Lawrence Hightower.

Shaking her head, she resolved to clear her thoughts and enjoy the moment.

His hand reached around her body and slowly caressed her pleasure point. Each circular motion co-incided with a thrust of his hips. He'd at least stopped talking, but the scandalous torture remained.

"Lawrence…" She couldn't take much more. And

no sooner did she think it than her body shook and convulsed.

She lost control of herself. She couldn't think. She could only feel.

He pulled out, scooped her from the desk and into his arms and carried her over to the sofa. Within seconds, she was on the comfy chocolate-brown sofa and he was in her again, sending her into orbit until they both found release together.

I love you. She wanted to say the words out loud, to scream them to the mountains surrounding them. But she couldn't. Not yet, maybe not ever.

When he came back from disposing of the protection, he scooped her up in his arms and carried her toward the bedrooms.

"Hey, what about dinner?" She squeaked out the question as her stomach dipped and tingles overtook her body.

"It can wait. I need to finish teaching you your lesson for keeping yourself away from me all day." He had a wickedly sexy gleam in his eyes and a sultry smile on his face.

She grinned. "Who knew being bad would make me feel so good?"

Chapter 12

After enjoying their meal together and having Lawrence shower her with praise for her culinary talents, she realized she could have listened to him rave about her cooking for the rest of her life. They could pull her feminist card if they wanted to, but she even let herself imagine preparing meals for handsome little boys who looked just like him as they all sat around a big table in a cute little house with a white picket fence.

Yes, she had it *that* bad.

And spending the rest of the evening in his arms having him make love to her with such passion and desire didn't help. Her body would never be the same. Her heart was lost forever.

And she had to leave him.

She bit her lip and wrung her hands as she watched him sleep.

David's harsh words reverberated in her head. If something were to happen to Lawrence because of her, she knew she wouldn't be able to handle it. It's bad enough that the McKnights were dead because they offered her a place of refuge. Lawrence couldn't die, too.

She thought about the two boyfriends who had ended up badly beaten. She remembered her brother with a hole in the middle of his forehead. Timmy and Tommy the same way. And then she imagined walking into the house and finding Lawrence shot, that handsome face drained of life, all because he tried to help her.

She closed her eyes and shook her head, trying to dispel the ugly image. A tear escaped and she wiped it away. He was too amazing a spirit to lose his life because of some foolishness she'd brought to his door.

She eased out of the bed, got dressed, grabbed his keys, wrote a brief note and left.

It was for the best in the end.

Lawrence rolled over and reached for Minerva. He was filled with so much need he thought he might burst. He realized he would probably never get enough of this sweet and sexy woman. He couldn't stop thinking about her; she had his mind. He couldn't stop desiring her; she had his body. He couldn't stop caring about her and wanting to keep her safe; she had his heart.

He slapped the cold empty space on the bed where her warm succulent body had been. Squinting at the clock, he saw that it was about 1:00 a.m. Where was she? He got out of bed in search of her and only started to get antsy when he reached the kitchen and saw the note on the refrigerator.

The note read *Sorry, Lawrence, but it's time for me to go. I'll leave the keys in the car for you in town at the bus station. Sorry... Minerva.*

His eyes narrowed into a sliver and his blood boiled to a steam.

She played me!

Picking up the phone, he dialed the town sheriff. He might not ever hear the end of this from Dale, the sheriff, or Jed his deputy. But he needed help catching Minerva before she got too far. And when he caught her, that would be it. He was taking her back to Paterson and handing her over. Let the department handle the little conniving woman.

The phone rang several times at the town's police station before anyone answered. He recognized Jed's voice right away and silently cursed his luck. If either of the two men were more prone to making sure Lawrence never forgot how the big-city detective needed the help of the small-town sheriff, it was Jed.

"Hey, Jed. This is Lawrence Hightower—"

"Hey, Hightower, I heard you were up at your family's place. Dale said you wanted us to look out for a white van. We haven't seen anything. A bit early in the season for you, isn't it?"

"Yeah. I'm actually here on business. We needed a safe house for a potential witness. That's the reason I'm calling. The witness is running scared. She actually took my truck and left a note saying she would leave the keys with it in town. I'm assuming she headed to the bus station. I can't let her get away."

"So you're saying you need us small-town officers to help you apprehend a potential witness that got away by taking your vehicle?"

Damn! "Yes, Jed. I would appreciate your help in this matter."

"Well, now, that's a first…" The sarcasm in Jed's voice pulsed through the phone lines.

Lawrence gritted his teeth and counted to ten. "I would be in debt to you and more than willing to pay it back however you see fit."

Damn! Wait until I get my hands on Minerva…

"Yeah? You'd be willing to take back every snide remark you ever made about small-town policing?"

"Of course. Those comments were made in the spirit of friendship." Lawrence forced a chuckle.

"Hmm… Well, I'm not saying that's what I want. But you'd best believe I'll be calling in the marker on this one, Hightower."

"Yeah, well, you have to actually find her first…"

"I'll give you a call when we get her. You want us to bring her back to you or take her into the station?"

"Maybe Minerva Jones needs a taste of how grave the situation is… Bring her into the station and let her get a feel for the cell."

"I guess that means you'll be needing a ride into town?"

Damn!

"Yeah, I guess so."

"She in your SUV? The black Navigator?"

"Yeah."

"Okay. See ya in a bit, Hightower." Jed chuckled. "I can't wait to share this with Dale. We're gonna have a good laugh about this one. And I'm sure we'll be able to think of a really creative way for you to pay us back."

I'm sure you will...

"Thanks again, Jed. See you soon."

Another cruddy jail cell?

When did this become her life?

The last thing she expected was the sheriff, or the deputy in this case, to come waltzing into the bus depot looking to arrest her. She hadn't factored in a long wait for the bus or the bus being late. But she should have, since they were in such a small Pennsylvania town.

The young deputy had a smirk on his face the entire time and mumbled something about big-city cops not being immune to pretty young things. She could only assume that Lawrence must have called them to find her. That's why she was so shocked when the Ashton Kutcher-looking deputy locked her in the holding cell.

The really messed-up part about it was that when the deputy came back in, with Lawrence right behind him, Lawrence's eyes said it all. He was pissed.

"I can see why you got sidetracked enough to lose your witness, Hightower. She's a pretty girl. I guess even a big-city cop like yourself can be a victim to a pretty face. Try to hold on to her this time." The deputy chuckled and patted Lawrence on the back before settling in at his desk. He eyed them both as if he were waiting for a show to begin.

"Thanks again, Jed. And like I said, I owe you."

"Yeah, and like I said, you'll pay." Jed chuckled.

Lawrence gritted his teeth and then his angry eyes landed on her.

Oh, yeah, this was going to be bad. Would she be able to get him to understand that she just didn't want anything bad to happen to him? How could she do that without letting him know how much she had come to care for him? She couldn't tell him she loved him. It would be too awkward, and she knew she wouldn't be able to deal with him not loving her back.

Unflinching, she toughened her resolve and looked him dead in the eye.

He narrowed his gaze and his nostrils flared. Not in that sexy, I-want-you-so-bad-I-could-hardly-breathe way that she had gotten used to over the past few days. No, this was the you're-lucky-you're-in-that-cell-or-I-would-throttle-you stare.

She couldn't help it; she flinched. So much for being tough… It was hard to put on airs when you knew you were wrong.

"Give me one good reason why I shouldn't press charges and have you arrested for grand theft auto,

Minerva." He bit the words out in a cold and distanced manner that made her heart stop.

Because I love you and I'm sorry hardly seemed like the right thing to say. She took a deep breath. "I—"

"I don't want to hear it. Jed, can you let Ms. Jones out. We'll be leaving now."

"Aww... And here I thought I'd be getting a front-row seat for this one. Oh, well..." Jed took his keys and let her out of the cell.

Lawrence was painfully silent during the ride back to the house. His jaw set in a harsh slant, he kept his eyes on the road and he seemed to have a tenuous grasp on calm.

"Lawrence—"

"Don't." He bit the word out, his tone demanding and resolute.

It would be the longest thirty minutes of her life. She couldn't possibly be expected to just sit there and not try to explain. Why did he care if she left anyway? It wasn't like she was going to steal his car. She had left a note.

"Listen, Lawrence, I know you're upset and I don't blame you—"

"Damn it, Minerva, I said don't! I don't want to hear it."

"Well, I need to explain! See, what had happened was..." She stopped talking when she noticed him putting his signal on and pulling off onto the shoulder. He stopped the car and put it in Park before turning and glaring at her.

Uh-oh. This can't be good. Maybe it wasn't the best time to try and explain.

She swallowed.

"I figured it would be best if I put more distance between myself and the people looking for me, before anyone else got hurt." She rushed out the words and chanced a glance at his face.

She'd seen stone more flexible than the angry glare on his face. She didn't remember ever seeing him that upset. Even when he was her permanent shadow and thought she was a drug-dealing gang banger, he'd never looked at her with the kind of disgust and distrust that he had on his face now. They had come so far only to end up further apart than they were in the beginning.

And it was all her fault.

"Lawrence—"

"Save it, Minerva. I don't want to hear your excuses. To think I even considered trying to trust you. You can't be trusted. I won't believe a word that comes out of your lying mouth."

He pulled back onto the road and she didn't bother trying to explain anymore.

When they got back to the house she figured she'd just go to her room and try not to cry. She'd been doing a wonderful job of keeping her emotions in check, given all the craziness that had happened in her life since her brother was murdered. So she couldn't really understand the sudden and overwhelming need she felt to crawl into a ball and bawl like a baby.

It was as if the world was crashing down on her—

her brother's murder, the McKnights' murder, David being angry with her and now Lawrence being angry with her, too.

The whirlwind of feelings threatening to combust inside her must have meant she was further gone than she thought. Having Lawrence so upset with her was breaking her heart and the only way that could happen was if she was already head over heels in love with him.

Feeling heaviness in her chest, she walked toward the room she had been sleeping in when she wasn't wrapped in Lawrence's arms in his bed.

"Where do you think you're going?"

"To my room."

"Uh-uh. Do I look stupid? You think I'm going to take my eyes off you now? All you'll do is try and sneak out again. We're sharing a room."

"I just thought, since you are so upset with me—"

"Oh, trust me, if I could be away from you right now I would. And you certainly don't have to worry about me trying anything with you. This is about the fact that I can't trust you and I will not give you another opportunity to flee."

A sharp pain raced through her chest. How many times was he going to say he couldn't trust her? Like that was something new.

He has one more time to throw that trust crap in my face, though. One more time…

"Can I at least get my nightgown?" She hadn't exactly needed one when she had shared his bed before.

"Hurry up. Don't let me have to come get you."

She put on her nightgown and went into his bedroom. The pink cotton oversize T-shirt-styled gown came past her knees, but she still felt a little underdressed. She stood by the bed for a moment wondering if he really wanted her to share the space with him.

The angry glint in his eyes made her weary of asking him if he really thought it was a good idea. Honestly, she didn't know if she could take much more of his snapping at her without cussing him out. And since she was in the wrong, she would try to stay away from giving him a piece of her mind.

As soon as she got into the bed, he walked over, took her arm and cuffed it to the bedpost.

Oh, now see…that's it! That's the last straw!

"What the hell are you doing, Lawrence? Is this really necessary?"

"Since you snuck your behind out of this very bed and this very room while I was sleeping, I'd say yes, it is necessary."

"You're acting like a real jerk right now." Her voice caught and she willed herself not to cry. It wasn't about trying to save face; it was about righteous indignation.

He shrugged and walked away. She watched him strip down to his boxers and get back into the bed. She willfully ignored his body.

"Who is David Sims, Minerva?" he asked in a clipped voice. His eyes were pinned on her.

She blinked.

Where the hell did that come from? How the hell does he know about David?

"And don't you dare lie!"

"I'm not going to, Lawrence. I messed up. I shouldn't have just left like that. But that doesn't mean you get to treat me like crap. I'm sorry."

"Save it, Minerva. Answer the question."

The way he asked the question showed he already knew something. So no matter how much she had wanted to keep David's name out of this and spare him from becoming more involved with her brother's mess, she had to at least offer up something to Lawrence.

"He was my brother's best friend and the McKnights' first cousin. We all grew up together, but David was the only one of their group not to get involved with gangs or lead a life of crime."

"If he's not a criminal, then why is the LAPD looking for him? And why is there a possibility that he was in New Jersey when the McKnights were murdered?"

"LAPD is dirty. The dirty cops working for the people who killed my brother might be after him. I told you that the people who killed my brother have dirty cops working for them. That's why I had to leave without talking to the police. I'm sure those same dirty cops are the ones trying to blame David. He's a businessman, not a criminal. It makes no sense."

"If you don't know who killed your brother and who might be after you, how do you know they have dirty cops on their payroll?"

"That's what I was told…"

"By who? Who told you that?"

"David told me… That's why he helped me. He gave me the money to leave town and he got Timmy and Tommy to let me hide out at their place."

"And you don't find it a little too coincidental that three people with ties to Sims are dead? That he was really the only one who knew where you were and he might have been in town when those people tried to snatch you and the McKnights were killed?"

"David wouldn't do that…"

"The Paterson Police Department found the people in the white van and they are close to getting them to finger who hired them. So far they're only saying it was a guy from California."

She nibbled on her lip. This was just too much.

Did David really have something to do with Calvin's death? Timmy and Tommy's, too? It couldn't be. Could it?

Her voice choked. "Why would he do that?"

"You're saying you don't know anything about David's criminal activities?"

"No. He's not… My brother always used to say that he was a schoolboy who couldn't hang… I…"

"We're going back to Paterson in the morning. We're going to put you under surveillance and we're going to find out once and for all what is going on with you, Minerva. If you're somehow involved with this Sims guy and his criminal activity, we'll find out."

"Oh, my God! You really think I'm a criminal?"

"I don't know what to think. I know innocent people don't sneak off and steal cars in the middle of the night."

A lump settled in her throat the size of a golf ball. Her eyes started to sting.

The murdered bodies of Calvin, Timmy and Tommy swam into her consciousness. She hadn't even buried her brother because she had trusted David to handle it. What if he hadn't? Was Calvin in a cheap pine box without so much as a grave marker?

She gasped and tried to bite back the sob that wouldn't be contained. She never knew she could hurt this badly. She turned around and faced the wall.

Lawrence had barely trusted her anyway and now he never would. Two men were dead for trying to help her and she'd failed at getting away so that she could get Lawrence out of danger. He could die. The stinging in her eyes heightened and intensified.

He cannot die.

The weight of everything—the death, the distrust, the denied desire—all converged and blew wide open the hole in her heart that had just started to close after her brother's death. The best thing she could do was try not to cry too loudly because the tears were determined to come, no matter how hard she tried to stifle them. She wouldn't be able to hold them back for long.

"And we also need to address our condom mishap a few days ago. You could be pregnant."

"Don't worry, *Detective*, I won't be bothering you if I am. You don't have to worry about me even telling you. I would hate to burden you with sharing a child with a woman you can't trust."

His hands gripped her shoulders and turned her to

face him. The arm cuffed to the bedpost twisted a little and she winced.

"Don't even think about it, Minerva. If you dare have my child and think you can just not let me know, you had better think again. Do not test me on this one. I will not have a child of mine out there in the world that I can't be a father to."

Everything was a mess and becoming messier with each passing minute. Could her heart break any more? What if she were pregnant? Could she really raise a child with Lawrence around as a constant reminder of how she ruined what could have been an amazing thing between them?

No.

"You can threaten me all you want. But I don't have to do anything but stay black and die. You can't make me tell you anything. You can't make me do anything I don't want to do."

His eyes narrowed and that hurtful, disgusted look suffused his entire face. "You just try it then, Minerva. Try having my child without letting me know. You'd better pray that I never find out you did, because your betrayal card is full with me already."

She closed her eyes. "I don't know why we're even talking about this, let alone arguing about it. I'm not going to argue about nonexistent issues." The thought that she might be pregnant and could possibly have a child by a man she loved who didn't trust her was the one extra thing—on top of her pent-up guilt over her brother, the McKnights' murder and Lawrence's life possibly being at risk—that finally broke her down. She couldn't hold in her feelings any longer.

She turned back around and her tears started almost immediately. The tears poured forth as if someone had opened up floodgates.

Lawrence thought he would be able to fall off to sleep with relative ease. After all, he had been right not to trust her all along. He should have felt vindicated. He should have been at ease with the knowledge that he had called it correctly. Instead, he felt like someone had stuck a knife in his heart, twisted it and left it in.

He could tell that she was trying to hold back tears, that the only thing stopping her from heart-wrenching sobs was her pride. It broke his heart to hear her cry and *that* angered him. Why should he even care? Her tears should be of no consequence to him at all. But they bothered him. His anger dissipated with each shudder of her breath, each shake of her shoulders, each soft sob.

"Minerva, stop. Don't cry. Please."

She kept crying.

"Look, I know you're upset that you got caught and couldn't get away, but crying isn't going to get you anywhere."

Plus, you're breaking my heart. Stop it please, baby.

He got up and unlocked the handcuffs before pulling her into his arms. As soon as he did, she let loose a cascade of tears and the silent crying became harsh, stuttering cries so filled with anguish and pain it shattered his soul.

She buried her head in his chest and sobbed.

This was the woman who took his constant surveillance with a smirk and a smart comment. This was the woman who took Kendall's interrogation without cracking. He hadn't seen her break into tears then, so why was she crying now?

Feeling like a class-A jerk, he rubbed her back.

"I'm sorry…Lawrence. I just didn't want anything to happen to you… I couldn't take it if anything happened to you…" Her words were stilted by soft gasps of breath.

Her words sounded so heartfelt. He lifted her chin and stared in her overflowing eyes. She seemed so sincere.

"It's okay, baby. Nothing is going to happen to me. And I'm not going to let anything happen to you, either. I promise. Now please stop crying, okay? Please."

"I can't because it's all messed up now. I just wanted to do the right thing because I care about you so much. So much… I care about you more than I wanna admit. And if you died because of me, it would kill me—"

"Nothing is going to happen to me. Don't worry yourself about that. I'm a cop. I can take care of myself. I'm a tough guy. The only thing I *can't* handle is your tears, so stop crying."

She didn't stop. So he held her and listened until she had spent all her tears. Holding her in his arms felt so right it scared him. There wasn't any question in his mind; she was "the one" for him.

Chapter 13

Waking up in Lawrence's strong arms made her feel safer than a girl on the run should feel. She almost wished she could stay in his embrace forever. Forget almost, she did wish she could stay there forever, *forever-ever*. She wanted this man for her very own and knowing she couldn't have him, because he would never be able to trust her and it was all her fault, darn near had her in tears again.

Toughen up, girlie!

She stretched and gazed up into his piercing, sexy brown eyes. They were so clear and determined, so sure. She figured the way she had bawled like a baby last night her own eyes must have been bloodshot and puffy.

"Good morning," he said in that strong sexy voice she had come to love.

"Morning…listen…I apologize for totally spazzing out on you last night. I don't know what came over me crying like that. Guess I must have sprung a leak." She tried for a joke to cover her embarrassment.

Yeah and a leak isn't the only thing sprung up in here. You're sprung! Sprung out over this sexy detective. In love? You better hope he doesn't figure it out.

"That's okay. Every woman is entitled to a good cry when she feels like it, even little tough girls like you, Minerva. I'm sorry I acted like such a jerk and—"

"It's okay. You were right to fly off. I shouldn't have left like that. I shouldn't have taken your car. I'm sorry—"

He brushed his lips across hers. The soft gentleness of his lips, coupled with the warm caring gaze of his eyes, was her undoing.

Why'd he have to do that? Why'd he have to kiss her and let her know how amazing he was? How perfect he would be for her if they had met under different circumstances. It wasn't going to work between them, not that she should have allowed herself to hope things could work anyway. It wasn't going to work and that broke her heart.

"Everything is going to be fine, baby. I promise you that. I care about you, too. And I'm not about to let anything or anyone hurt you. Not even me…" He brushed his lips across hers again and the kiss intensified within seconds.

He cared about her.

She tried to push back the ever-growing hope in her heart but she couldn't do it. She opened herself to her feelings as surely as she opened her mouth to his. Wrapping her arms around his neck she pulled him closer and poured her heart and soul into her kiss.

The desire between them refused to be contained. It was unwieldy and followed a law of its own.

He kissed her deeply before answering. "I care about you. A lot. So much it scares me." He covered her lips again and their tongues danced.

She let her hand roam his muscular frame and imagined she'd be able to hold on to every ripple, every bulge for the rest of her life. She let herself believe he was her man. That he would *always* be her man.

And when he touched her, she couldn't help but melt. She was so caught up that she barely noticed her nightgown coming off. But she couldn't help but notice when he slipped on the protection and entered her. The stroke was so sure, so strong that she had to pay attention.

"Ahhhh…" Her body shook and her legs trembled. This was what perfection felt like.

"Yes, baby… You're mine and I'm not going to let anything happen to you. *Ever*." He moved his hips with a slow determination that set off triggers inside her.

Triggers of desire. Triggers of passion. Triggers of emotion.

It felt like someone had placed a packet of Pop Rocks in some seltzer water and placed it in her heart.

She couldn't keep up with everything he was making her feel. The only thing she could do was hold on.

As she moved her hips to meet his thrusts, which seemed to increase in pace with each minute, she wished she could tell him how much she loved him.

"Minerva..."

The way he said her name made her heart do flip-flops. He made her name sound so sexy, so desirable. He made her love her name. She'd never go by M. Athena again as long as he was around to say her name.

"Say that again... Say my name again..." She swiveled her hips and pressed her pelvis against his, trying to meld herself to him.

He smiled and lifted her leg so that it rested on his shoulder. He began a slow torturous thrusting, reaching deeper than he ever had. "Minerva...Minerva... Minerva..."

Everything inside of her exploded and she screamed. He smiled again and lifted her other leg to his shoulder. "Minerva..."

She couldn't stop shaking. It was a good thing he was holding on to her. She didn't think she could take much more.

"Minerva..."

"Okay...okay... Please..."

He moved quickly in and out, over and over again. "Please what, baby? What do you want me to do? Whatever you want baby, just ask me..."

Her head was spinning and her heart threatened to burst right out of her chest. Her sex tightened around him and she screamed again as he said her name and they both found release.

In the aftermath, as he held her, she made her wish. She wanted to stay there with him, just like this.

"We need to shower and hit the road, baby. We have to catch the person who's after you."

By the time they actually got going, it was early in the evening. They didn't have any daylight hours, but it didn't matter. Because the time they had spent making love and straightening up the vacation home was time she knew she would remember forever. In fact, if her time with Lawrence was about to end, she wanted to eke out as many memories as she possibly could.

The ride back felt so much calmer than the ride there had been. They talked, cracked jokes and laughed. Her guard was completely down. But in the back of her mind she knew she would regret being so lax. Her heart had never been so compromised.

"…And that's what happens when keeping it real goes horribly wrong…" Lawrence burst out laughing at his own joke.

Pushing back the creeping fear that threatened to overtake her, she let out an exaggerated sigh at his corniness.

"Aww…you know that was funny. You know you want to laugh."

"*Whatever.* Don't quit your day job, dude. You certainly won't be giving Dave Chappelle a run for his money anytime soon," she teased.

"See how much you know! I actually got the joke from a DVD of Chappelle's Show."

"Well, then it must really all be in the delivery, because, you, sir, are so-oo *not* funny." Pushing her worries to the back of her mind, she plastered a grin on her face. "Okay, check this one out. There was a family driving along the highway and they picked up this guy who was hitchhiking. He had a big black bag with him and it made the wife nervous. She asked him what was in the bag. And he said, 'None of your damn business.' They drove for a while and it started to *really* make her nervous.

"So she asked again, and again he replied, 'None of your damn business.' Finally the husband said, 'Listen, buddy, if you don't let us know what's in the bag I'm gonna have to put you out.' And the hitchhiker was like 'Whatever, fine, put me out.' So they stop at a gas station and put him out and wouldn't you know it he left the big black bag in the car. Of course the couple couldn't help it. They *had* to look." She stopped and glanced out the window waiting for Lawrence to give her the opening for her punch line.

"What was in the bag?"

"None of your damn business!" She slapped her knee and howled out her laughter. As she turned to him, she noticed his lips twist in mock disdain as he shook his head.

"That was so corny. You have the nerve to talk about me when you are telling jokes like that? Girl, please."

"Aww…you're just mad because you wanted to know what was in the bag." She chuckled at her own joke.

"Okay, let's just agree that we both suck at telling jokes and resist the urge to try to get a laugh."

"Maybe you, but I'm funny. I got jokes for days."

He laughed. "That was the funniest thing you've said yet."

She slapped her knee again in mock laughter. "Ah, ha, ha, ha...*not* funny."

"So, are you ready to do what we need to do to catch Sims?"

"Do you really think that he killed my brother? I mean that's a lot for me to believe. He helped me when he didn't have to, Lawrence."

"He helped you what? Leave town when you should have gone to the police? Why would he want to keep you from talking to the police? Think about it."

"Because he knew I didn't see anything and it didn't make sense to put my life in danger when I had no information to share. He was trying to help me because he was my brother's best friend."

"And he called you recently trying to find out where you were, right?"

"Because he's worried about me." She didn't want to believe that David was a murderer, a criminal. What would that say about her judgment? It would confirm her brother's constant statements about how she wasn't made for the 'hood and would never survive on her own without him. She'd always thought Calvin had used that just to control her and keep her close, but if what Lawrence was saying was true...

"Has he called back again?"

"I turned my cell phone off."

"Turn it back on."

She pulled the phone out of her purse and turned it on. She'd missed twenty calls since she had turned it off, and there were six messages. She dialed her voice mail and her heart stilled.

If David sounded angry when she spoke to him, his messages ran the gamut. He'd gone from calm and apologetic to angry and violent. The last couple of messages had gotten progressively louder and more threatening.

Lawrence pulled off the highway and into a rest stop. He took the phone from her. As he listened to the messages, his face grew increasingly angry. He gave the phone back to her and dialed his own cell phone.

"Kendall, any more information on Sims? And is the safe house ready?" He paused and rolled his eyes. "Hello, *Chief*. We're on our way back to Paterson. We're about a half hour away. I'm ready to catch this fool."

He tapped the wheel as he listened to the chief of police.

She wished could hear both sides of the conversation. Could it really be possible? Was David a killer? And if he was, why didn't he just kill her when he killed her brother? Why send her to Jersey? It made no sense.

"Well, I hope we can set up something, by tomorrow the latest. I'll just keep her at my place until you can set it up." He paused, shaking his head emphatically.

"Nah. That's not gonna happen. I'll watch out for her. And I want to be close by at the safe house, too."

He let out a hiss of air. "I'm not trying to call the shots or tell you how to do your job, Chief. I'm just hoping that you'll let me look out for her since we've already built a rapport."

Mmmm, she thought, *is that what they're calling it these days...*

"All right, thanks." He was about to hang up and he stopped. "Huh? That's tonight? Oh, damn, that is tonight. Thanks for reminding me. My brother and my mother would have a fit if I missed that. I guess I'll see you tonight. It should be safe to bring her. There'll be so many cops and firemen in the place that no criminal in his right mind would try and roll up in there. See you later."

Lawrence turned to her. "So it looks like you might have to spend yet another night in my glowing company, and we're going to a surprise birthday party for my sister-in-law, Penny. It's tonight."

"Are you sure that's a good idea? I mean I could just go to a hotel or something. I don't want to infringe on your family time or your personal space."

"You won't be. I want you to come. And I have no problem sharing my personal space with you. I'm looking forward to it actually." A sly grin graced his face, and she had to shake her head.

"Yeah, I bet you wouldn't have a problem with that. But what if I did?"

"What? Are you sick of me already? And here I thought you couldn't get enough of Big Papa."

She guffawed.

"Harsh on the ego, aren't you?" He chuckled. "Good thing I know how you really feel."

"So tell me, Big Papa," she said jokingly with a sexy lilt in her voice. "How *do* I really feel?"

"You think I'm the most handsome man on the planet and the best lover in the universe. And you like me…you like me a *lot*."

She grinned and then twisted up her lips in mock defiance before giving him a serious side-eye look. "You *a'right*."

"That's not what you were screaming a few hours ago, baby."

"Well, I wouldn't know what I was screaming… Couldn't hear for all your moaning, groaning and yelling…"

He laughed. "Okay, you got that one right. But, anyway, back to what I was saying. I'd love for you to accompany me to the surprise party, and spending another night with you is not a hardship, baby."

She glanced down at her outfit. She was wearing a pair of brown slacks and a sort of hip and funky brown, taupe and cream blouse with the stiletto-heeled boots she'd been wearing during her undercover stint. It turned out that they looked a lot cuter with her business casual-style clothing than she would have thought. "Am I dressed okay?"

"You look beautiful."

"Okay, then. I'd love to go to the party."

Chapter 14

Lawrence couldn't keep his eyes off Minerva. No one could have told him, when he first saw her on his beat three months ago, that he would fall for her the way he had.

The party was actually just what they both needed. After several days with only each other to talk to and be with, being around a crowd was probably a good thing. Too bad the only thing he really wanted to do was be with her. Alone.

"So who's the girl?" Jason nodded across the room to where Minerva was chatting with the women in their family.

The women, led by his mother, Celia Hightower, had pretty much converged on Minerva the moment they walked in. It was the first time Lawrence had brought a woman to a family gathering, and he guessed that his mother was trying to figure out everything she could about Minerva.

"Yeah, since when did you start bringing a date to family functions? This is new. She must be special." Joel leaned against the wall and offered his two cents.

"So who is she? You'd better get her from over there by Mom. She'll have you walking down the aisle in no time. Look at what happened with these two clowns." Patrick rolled his eyes in mock disgust at Joel and Jason.

Lawrence frowned. His brothers had seen Minerva before. "Don't you guys remember her from a few months back, at the happy hour. She was hanging with the McKnights?"

"The criminal chick?" Joel scrunched up his eyebrows as he stared across the floor at Minerva.

"She's not a criminal." Lawrence shook his head.

"That's her? Dang, she looks different. Didn't she have wilder hair? And wasn't she pissed off at you for arresting her? Why would she even come to the party with you?" Jason also stared as he took in all the changes.

"He arrested her? So what are you doing? You're bringing criminals to the party? What the hell is wrong with you?" Patrick snapped.

"You dating criminals now?" Joel offered with a smirk. "Dang, bro, are times that hard? I would have thought with Jason and me off the market, old guys like you and Patrick would have more opportunities—not less."

He groaned. At this rate, he wouldn't make it through the night. "She's not a criminal. And we're not dating." *Not exactly dating...* They were so much more and yet... "And for the record, you two being out of the game could never have an impact on a player like me. We weren't even in the same league. I was light-years ahead of y'all."

Did he just talk about his player skills in the past tense? He wasn't even going to touch it.

"Okay, if you're not dating her, then why is she here with you?" Patrick twisted up his lips in disbelief. "Am I going to be the only one who will be able to resist and remain single? You clowns are dropping like flies, one by one. I refuse to go out like that."

Lawrence explained as much of the situation to his brothers as he could without kissing and telling. He decided it was best to leave those parts out. But he did fill them in on the threats to Minerva and how he wasn't going to let anything happen to her.

When he was done, his brothers were each nodding their heads.

"If you need anything, any help at all, bro, you got it." Jason offered with a genuine expression on his face.

"Yeah, man, if I can do anything let me know. That poor girl has been through a lot. And if she's cool with you, she's cool with me." Joel patted him on the back.

"I'm here if you need me, too. But be careful. Be sure you know exactly who she is this time. She came into town pretending to be someone she clearly wasn't and who's to say that this incarnation is the real her." Patrick's face had softened a little but he still had his underlying guard up.

Watching her talk and laugh with his mother and the other women, Lawrence knew in his heart he was looking at the real her. And he also knew he wanted her in his life. Forever.

"This is my girl! My girl…umm…umm…" Carla snapped her fingers trying to remember Minerva's name.

"Minerva." Minerva nervously glanced across the beautifully decorated hall in the Elks Lodge to where Lawrence was standing chatting with his brothers as she helped Carla remember her name.

She'd never been to a surprise birthday party like this before. The small hall was decked out with lots of flowers, balloons and streamers. Everyone was dressed to impress and having a great time.

"Minerva…Minnie! That's right. My girl! What you doing coming up in here with Lawrence? The last time I saw y'all together you looked like you wanted to cut him. Oooo, y'all shoulda seen it. He came up in the Laundromat beasting after her like Jason used to be beasting after your Penny when you first came home, remember?" Carla's neck moved as she spoke with barely contained excitement.

"Really, that's interesting." Celia Hightower smiled, as she looked Minerva over. "How long have you been seeing my son?"

"Oh, we're not seeing each other, really, we…well… he's just watching out for me until they catch the murderers." She explained as much of her situation with Lawrence as she could to them without letting them know how much he had rocked her world.

"Oh, you poor girl. You've had a rough few months." Celia hugged her.

"My girl is tough, she can hang. Y'all shoulda seen her in the Laundromat, she all but ran Lawrence out of there." Carla's voice seemed to fill the room.

"Really?" Penny's eyebrow arched as she grinned.

Minerva thought that Penny looked very familiar and couldn't help staring at the beautiful woman. It was only when she smiled that she realized where she knew Penny from. She was the former video girl, Penny Keys. Calvin used to have posters and calendars with Penny Keys's scantly clad pictures all over the walls in his bedroom. He used to say he was going to marry Penny Keys one day. It was between Penny Keys and another hot video model at that time, Maritza Morales. Minerva used to wish she would grow up and fill out in the way that those women were built. She had developed a cute shape, but it was nothing to rival the tall, shapely video girls.

Penny Hightower still held her breathtaking beauty. The hair that used to be long and chemically processed now flowed down her back in curly sisterlocks. Her soft brown skin now radiated a vibrant expectant mother glow. And even with her very pregnant belly sticking out, she still had an amazing shape. Her copper eyes sparkled with warmth and friendship.

"I would have liked to have seen that one. Between Lawrence and Patrick, I don't know which Hightower brother is more surly." Samantha, Joel's fiancée, shook her head as she laughed.

Samantha had the kind of earthy beauty that radiated from within and spread outward, touching everyone she came in contact with. Her silky chocolate skin was flawless and her jet-black natural hair was in neat twists and hung just past her shoulders. She also had one of those grown-woman figures that Minerva now knew she would never have.

If these were the kind of women that the Hightower men married, then her petite frame probably didn't stand a chance. These women had boobies for days, hips and long legs. She was a member of the itty-bitty-titty committee. And while she had a nice round behind and hips, it was very much in proportion with her height and size. She didn't have a booming booty, as she remembered her brother and his friends calling them back in the day. She thought back to Lawrence's comments in the Laundromat about her not being his type.

"Well, until a certain physical therapist came into Joel's life, your fiancé might have given Patrick and Lawrence a run for their money in that contest," Penny said jokingly.

"Oh, the same could be said for Jason until you came along, Penny," Celia offered with a smile.

"And look at Lawrence now. He can barely keep his eyes off Minerva." Samantha's eyes gleamed with mischief.

"That's because he probably thinks I'm gonna run off." Minerva laughed lightly.

"Oh, Lawrence is probably my most slow-to-trust child. But once a person earns his trust and love, they'll have it for life. He's the most like his father in that regard. So it seems fitting that he would fall for you."

"He hasn't fallen for me, Mrs. Hightower. I mean… well…I just think he wants to help to do the right thing that's all…"

"And he had to take you all the way to the Poconos for that? Girl, they could have put you into any number of safe houses around the city or the county for that. And he brought you to a family gathering? Trust me. Even if my son is too dense to get it yet, he's into you without a doubt."

"I think I'd have to agree with you on that one, Mama Celia." Penny nodded.

"Me, too. He can't keep his eyes off her and he has that *look* on his face." Samantha giggled.

"Yeah, the let-me-make-sure-she-doesn't-flee look. The let-me-make-sure-she-doesn't-make-one-false-move-so-I'd-have-to-arrest-her look." Minerva laughed even though it was the last thing she felt like doing. "I'm sorry to burst your bubbles, but the only *look* Detective Lawrence Hightower is giving me is the look that a cop gives a suspect. The man thinks I'm the guiltiest woman to walk the planet."

"When you're dealing with a Hightower man, especially a Hightower cop, sometimes you *are* guilty. Guilty of stealing his heart… And he can't keep his eyes off you because he's too busy trying to figure out how you did it." Celia laughed. "One day, I'm gonna have to tell you ladies the story about how I met my James. Let's just say that Minerva and I may have a lot in common. But tonight is not about me. It's about the birthday girl."

Penny patted her pregnant belly. "Uh-uh, you can't drop that tantalizing bit of information on us and expect us to just let it go. We want the goods."

"Maybe another time." Celia glanced around the room. "I sure hope Sophie doesn't decide to crash the party. It's been nice and quiet around lately since we banned her from family gatherings."

"If she knows what I know, she'll stay away. I still owe her a butt kicking from Penny's wedding. She would not want to come up in my baby's birthday party acting like she acts." Carla's face took on a scowl.

"Who is this Sophie?" Minerva asked, noticing the sour expressions that came over all the women's faces as soon as Celia mentioned the woman's name.

"She's Celia's sister-in-law. She's pretty much a snob who thinks no woman is good enough for the Hightower name. And she will go out of her way to be insulting and try to sabotage your relationship if she thinks you and Lawrence are getting serious. She'll do it just because she's pretty much evil. She's hated me since I was a kid. She tried to get Samantha fired from her job and she has given Mama Celia the blues for years. But you don't have to worry. You won't have to deal with her tonight. I think she'd rather die than attend a party thrown in my honor." Penny rolled her eyes in disgust through most of her rant, but at the end she had a big grin on her face.

Minerva assumed that grin was because Sophie wasn't coming to the party. She made a mental note to try to stay out of this Sophie woman's way. It wasn't as if she'd be around for long anyway, or as if she and Lawrence had a relationship for the woman to sabotage.

"Well, enough of talking about meddlesome kill-joys. I'm going to find my husband for a nice dance." Celia Hightower shimmied her shoulder and did a little spin before walking away.

"Me, too." Carla took off in search of Gerald.

"I guess I can spare a dance for my fine husband since he pulled off this big surprise without me knowing it." Penny didn't seem like she needed a lot of convincing at all.

"Yeah, I have a few Beyoncé moves for my fiancé, with his fine self." Samantha danced her way after the rest of the women.

Minerva watched the women make their way across the floor to the men and head off to the small dance floor. The room was packed with friends and family and the entire thing felt more than a little overwhelming. The fact that Lawrence had this much family to call his own added one more thing to the growing list of reasons why he was out of her league. She had no family left. And the one person she had thought was close was the person Lawrence believed to be her brother's murderer.

"Would you like to dance?"

She looked up to find an extremely handsome guy standing beside her. He had a caramel complexion and the most vibrant hazel eyes she'd ever seen. She had a feeling she had better tell this wavy-haired brother no. But everyone else was on the dance floor having a great time. Lawrence probably wasn't going to ask her to dance. And she liked dancing. So she followed him out onto the dance floor.

Playing was a fast R & B track by one of those teenybopper boy singers, who did more sliding around and grinding sans shirt than actually singing. It was fun to just sway with the rhythm and pretend she didn't have a care in the world.

"So what's your name? And how do you know my best friend, Penny?"

"My name is Minerva. And I actually just met Penny. I'm here with Lawrence, her brother-in-law. Do you know him?"

"Sure do. I pretty much grew up in that house. My other best friend is his brother, Penny's husband, Jason. Penny, Jason and I have been friends ever since we were kids. They used to call us the Three Musketeers." He smiled at the memory.

"Really? That's cool you all managed to remain friends all this time. What's your name, by the way?"

"My name is Terrell. So you're here with Lawrence, huh? I'd better cut this dance short. I don't want him to come over here and put me in my place or anything like that."

"Please, it's not like that." She giggled even though her heart wanted it to be exactly like that.

"If you say so. But it looks like he's found a dance partner. Hmm… Interesting choice." There was a slight bristle in Terrell's voice that hadn't been there before.

She turned and saw that Lawrence was on the dance floor with a drop-dead-gorgeous woman. A tall, shapely woman with beautiful glossy black curls cascading down her back. She looked like she was either biracial or maybe Latina. She moved to the music like a woman who knew exactly what to do with her body.

Minerva plastered a smile on her face and turned back to Terrell. "See, I told you that you had nothing to worry about. Lawrence seems too busy to be concerned about what we're doing." *The jerk!*

She chanced another glance at the woman. She looked familiar. When Minerva looked at her face, she realized where she had seen her before. She was Maritza Morales, the other video model whose picture had graced Calvin's walls.

"That's Maritza Morales, the former video girl, right?"

"Yep. She's a business partner of Penny's. They own an image-consulting firm. I'm a silent partner in their business."

"Really? That seems cool."

"I'm also a record company executive."

"Wow! That must really be exciting." She tried to keep her eyes on Terrell and away from Lawrence and the beautiful Maritza. And she was doing a great job of it until the music slowed down and Lawrence and Maritza ended up right next to them on the dance floor.

Just as Terrell started to pull her closer, Lawrence reached for her. "You don't mind if we switch partners, do you, Terrell? I want to dance with my baby now."

"I don't want to dance with *him!*" Maritza screeched.

"Shut up, Maritza." Terrell pulled Maritza into his arms and danced her away.

Lawrence wrapped her in his arms and held her close as they swayed to Luther Vandross's "If Only for One Night." She tried to block out how apt the song seemed to be and how it foreshadowed the absolute and inevitable end of whatever it was they were doing.

"Your *baby?*" She slanted her eye and twisted her lip as she glanced up at him.

"That's right, Minerva. *Mine.* Terrell is lucky he's a family friend and my sister-in-law and mother would have my head if I hurt him."

"You're crazy… Absolutely nuts…" She couldn't help but giggle as she let herself relax in his arms. She wished they had more than one night, more than a few breathtaking days of bliss in the Poconos, more than a brief affair that she would never forget. But she was determined to eke out the most of what she could from her time with him. Once she was at the safe house, she probably wouldn't see him much at all.

"I'm crazy about you, baby. And don't you forget it."

He brushed his lips across her forehead and she shivered.

"I'm gonna miss you."

"Miss me? I'm not going anywhere. And neither are you." He slanted his eyes. "Don't play me, Minerva. No more trying to run away. Or, I promise you, I will lock you up and throw away the key."

"I'm not going to run away. I'm talking about once this is all over, once you catch the criminals—"

"I'm still not going anywhere. And neither are you."

"I have a life in California…" Technically, she didn't anymore.

He frowned. "We'll cross that bridge when we get to it. You ready to go? I'm thinking we both need to get a good night's rest. Things might get hectic pretty fast, and I want to be sharp. I said I wouldn't let anything happen to you and I meant it."

"We can go if you'd like. I think your family is really nice. I'd be cool with staying a little longer. At least until Penny cuts her cake… She was really surprised when she walked in with Carla. I can't believe Penny Keys and Maritza Morales are here. My brother would have loved this party."

"Yeah, well, Penny Keys is Penny Hightower now and your brother would have had to love her from afar. And even though Terrell and Maritza are fighting it, they are as good as a couple."

"Is that why he seemed to stiffen up when you stepped on the dance floor with her?"

Lawrence laughed. "Yep. He had my baby on the

dance floor, so I had to get his attention. And don't act like he was the only one shooting daggers. I saw your face when you looked at us. You need to go ahead and admit it. You were heated. Weren't you?"

"Well, she was more your type, wasn't she? *Taller, shapelier, crime-free…*" She tossed his words back lightly, even though remembering them made her heart feel heavy.

He stared at her for several seconds before speaking. "Guess I didn't really know what my type was until a certain little two-toned hair, mouthy, smart-aleck, incredibly sexy woman came my way."

Her heart thudded loudly in her chest. She had to get off the dance floor before she started believing in and wishing for forever in his arms. Luckily, they were about to cut the cake.

"Penny's cutting her birthday cake now. Let's go get a piece."

"Yeah, let's do that." He kept his arms around her as they walked off the dance floor.

She never wanted him to let her go.

The rest of the evening went by in a blur. His family was so nice and they all embraced her with open arms. Their closeness highlighted to her all the more why she and Lawrence couldn't really be together. Even when she wasn't playing little miss ghetto girl with the two-toned hair, even when she was her regular, recent college graduate, striving self, the Hightower family was still way out of her league.

And as she entered Lawrence's spectacular home,

she really felt out of place. He had the second-floor apartment in his refurbished two-family colonial home and rented out the first floor. The hardwood floors gleamed in the stunning home and the built-in amenities took her breath away. Like the family vacation home in the Poconos, Lawrence's place was decorated in warm and inviting earth tones.

The furniture was sleek, top of the line, and screamed bachelor pad. The dark-chocolate leather sofas had an ergonomic design to them as did the wood and glass tables that were stained to match the rich tones of the sofas.

"I love your place." She hoped her eyes weren't bugging out of her head as she took in the decorations and artwork in his home. "You collect black art." It was more of a statement than a question.

"Yes. I've been collecting for a while. A lot of the pieces at the vacation home are mine also. I don't have enough wall space here for my love of art."

"You have some lovely pieces." She noted he had many signed limited-edition prints and even some originals. His collection put the framed reprints from the little spot in the mall that hung on her Los Angeles apartment wall to shame. Yet another reason why they wouldn't work… While she fully intended to own this kind of original art when she finished her MSW and got on with her career, it was clear that because of their age difference and class difference, he was already where she had yet to be.

He pulled her into his arms as they walked down the

hallway to his bedroom and planted a kiss on her. Her lips tingled and came to life.

She didn't know how he did it, how he sparked something deep and passionate inside her with just a touch. And at that moment she didn't want to question it. She just wanted to bask in it, glow with it, let it flow and bathe in it.

She moaned and he lifted her up, carrying her the rest of the way and laying her gently on the bed. He made quick work of their clothing and protected them before entering her in one smooth, devastating stroke.

"Ahhhhhhh…." Her back arched and her head tilted back in reaction to the fullness she felt. Her heart stalled, stuttered and then pumped fiercely.

His mouth covered hers and he stole the breath she had been struggling so hard to hold on to. His tongue mimicked the sure and steady piston of his hips. And she lifted her hips to meet him thrust for thrust.

She wanted so badly to tell him she loved him. The words sat on the tip of her tongue almost refusing to be confined, daring her to defy their power, their inevitability. Even without saying the words, her heart knew what it felt and there was no going back.

He trailed kisses down her neck and took her nipples in his mouth one after the other after the other, making her body sing with each suckle, with each thrust.

"I want you to stay with me."

She opened her eyes and gazed at him. Did he just ask her to stay?

"I want you to stay with me, baby. Please."

His lips swooped down again, claiming her mouth.

How could she deny him anything when he kissed her like that? But she had to. Didn't she? She couldn't stay with him. That was crazy.

"Tell me you'll stay with me. Tell me, Minerva. Baby, please."

His hips seemed to take on a life of their own, indeed a mind of their own. They swiveled and swirled and pulled him out until only the tip was left before diving back in over and over again. Each move called her scream closer. It built up slowly in the pit of her stomach and then exploded into a high-pitched shriek.

He grinned and his expression seemed to say *I've got you now!*

"Stay." Withdraw.

"With." Thrust.

"Me." Withdraw.

"Please." Thrust.

He emphasized his words and with the movements of his hips.

Good. Lord.

The man was clearly bent on getting her compliance or driving her out of her mind with lust. She thought it must have been the latter because she was close to proclaiming her undying love for him and telling him that she would stay with him forever. And she could not proclaim her love. She just couldn't. No matter how much her heart felt like it was going to burst. No matter how many tears of joy threatened to spill. Her feelings had to remain her little secret.

She closed her eyes and kept up with his rhythm as best she could. She didn't want to look at him. Looking at him reminded her that she didn't have forever in his arms.

Determined, he kept up his sensuous assault, slowly driving her insane.

"Look at me, baby." He whispered the words in her ear, taking a nip as he finished his demand.

She shook her head and kept her eyes closed. She felt her sex tighten and release and could have sworn she saw stars lighting up the darkness. The bright boldness of her orgasm made her eyes spring open as a scream poured from the depths of her stomach to the tip of her tongue and out into the room.

He caught her in his gaze and he stilled. "I want us to explore this relationship without all the drama going on. Once we catch the person who killed the McKnights and tried to kidnap you, I want you to give us a shot. I want you to stay. Tell me that you'll stay."

He licked her bottom lip and nibbled. "Stay with me."

She didn't trust herself to open her mouth. If she did at that moment, with him looking so genuine and true, she would have told him that she loved him. Her heart was full of love and no longer content to hold it inside. So she slowly nodded.

"Is that a yes? You'll stay?"

She nodded again and he captured her mouth in a soul-stealing kiss.

Then he moved. Slow at first and then faster. His strokes were mind-blowing, atmosphere-altering.

"I'm glad you're staying with me, baby. So glad." He kissed her again.

"Lawrence!" She screamed his name and then bit her tongue not to say more. *I love you. I love you so much.* She wanted to say the words. She wrapped her hands around his neck and pulled his head down, taking his lips with her own.

He held her tight as they both found their release.

He kissed her on the forehead before getting up to remove the protection. When he came back he wrapped her in his arms and kissed her again. The smile on his face made her heart burst wide open. She bit her lower lip to keep quiet.

"I really am glad you've decided to stay in Jersey when this is all done. I think you'll find several great MSW programs at the universities here. You could probably even go to school full-time, since you won't have to worry about a roof over your head or anything like that."

Her eyes widened. "Huh?"

"I got you, baby. I want you to be able to reach your goals while we figure this thing out between us."

"So you want me to be a kept woman?"

"Not a kept woman. I just want you." He pulled her close. "And I want you to be happy and have everything you ever hoped for."

"But I can't just stay here and let you take care of me, Lawrence."

"Hey, you promised me just now that you would stay. I'm holding you to it."

"I may stay in New Jersey. But I don't want to become a leech. I can find my own place maybe…once things are all settled…and we can…ah…we can still see each other if you want…"

"I want…" He kissed her lips softly.

"I want you." He let his tongue trail the outline of her mouth.

"I want you here with me." He deepened his kiss, consuming her breath, taking everything.

He pulled away and gazed at her. "I'm not letting you go. But if you feel like you want to do something nice like make me one of your delicious meals every now and then, I won't complain."

She laughed. "I knew it. You don't want me. You want my cooking!"

He gaze turned serious. "I want the whole package. I want all of you, Minerva Athena Jones."

You already have all of me… She bit back the words in her mind and snuggled into his embrace. He wanted her, but he hadn't said that he loved her. She couldn't put her heart on the line if she didn't know for sure.

They sat in the safe house, a one-story home on the outskirts of town, with Detective Victor Morales from Los Angeles, members of the DEA and members of the homicide division of the Paterson Police Department.

"I got this package from an anonymous source last week and we've been trying to arrest David Sims ever since." Detective Morales, who actually turned out to be the video model Maritza Morales's older brother, took a seat in front of her. "Apparently, your brother wanted it to be mailed only if something happened to both you and him. When you disappeared for months, whoever Calvin paid to mail the information must have assumed you met with foul play."

"There's enough evidence in here to get David Sims on drugs, racketeering and a host of other crimes." The redheaded DEA agent, Donald Fitzpatrick, kept his green eyes fixed on her.

"But we want to get him on murder, as well. That's where your helping us can come in," Jennings, the guy from Paterson's homicide division hedged.

"She's not going to be used as bait!" Lawrence snapped.

"Does she want the man who killed her brother to pay for it? She's the only person he will come out of hiding for. We already have the person in place to leak the information. In exchange for leniency, your Detective Johnson has agreed to call Sims with the location of the safe house. We'll all be right here in the garage, listening, videotaping and waiting for him to confess. We'll get him on everything," Fitzpatrick stated.

"Johnson was dirty and working with Sims?" Lawrence shook his head.

Minerva could only shake her head. Well, at least she had called that one properly. She had known Detective Johnson was no good.

All the information made her head spin, but she knew what she had to do. For her brother. For her future. "I'll do it. You can use me as bait."

"No." Lawrence shook his head. "We can find another way to catch him."

"If he killed my brother and the McKnights, I want to be the one to catch him. Have Johnson make the call."

Chapter 15

Her roiling stomach, and the piercing ache she felt in her gut, stopped her from feeling safe and secure no matter how many cops and DEA agents were in the garage next door listening in. She had been duped for years. And what did that say about her? Was she that bad a judge of character? How could she not have known? Why had she been fooled by his clean-cut business manner?

She had been sitting around the safe house bored and not able to be with Lawrence for a couple of days before David finally took the bait and showed up. She answered the door, sincerely hoping that the cops next door were really ready to step in if things got bad.

"David, what are you doing here?"

"I could ask you the same thing. What the hell are you doing here? Did your little cop boyfriend put you up in this little spot? Are you playing live-in whore to the pigs now?"

He had an ugly expression on his face, almost crazed. She had never seen him like this and at that moment she knew David had killed her brother.

"Why are you in New Jersey, David?"

He hauled off and slapped her, catching her before she hit the ground. He dragged her into the living room.

Her head was spinning. The force of his blow made her see stars. She pulled away from him and slapped him back with everything in her.

"What did you hit me for? What is wrong with you?" Tears streamed down her face and they just made her angry. She didn't want to give him the benefit of her tears.

"Asshole. Don't you ever put your hands on me again."

He grabbed her arm and gave her a shake. "And if you don't stop asking me questions like that, I'll smack the shit out of you again. I'm asking the questions, here. Your ass is answering them. You got that?" He shook her again before flinging her on the sofa.

She blinked and bit back her retort. The taste of blood in her mouth made her wary of upsetting him further.

"So you were with that cop the entire time I've been here looking for you?"

She took a deep breath, but she didn't respond.

"Answer me, bitch, or you'll be swallowing your teeth."

"Yes. I was with him. What's it to you?"

He backhanded her again and her head bounced against the back of the sofa. She reared up and lifted her hand reflexively, coming close to slapping him back. The sinister expression on his face stopped her.

"You're smarter than this, baby girl. Don't make me hurt you. Now, ask me another question if you want to."

Where were the freaking cops? They needed to come in before he really hurt her.

"Did you give it up to him? You let him hit it?"

She rolled her eyes. How did she ever think this crass jerk had any semblance of class? She folded her arms across her chest.

He smirked. "You'd better answer the question."

"It's none of your business, David. I don't have—"

The next blow knocked her off the sofa and onto the floor. She could feel the blood coming from her nose and her mouth. This wasn't good.

"I'm sorry, David. Please don't hit me again. What did I…" She remembered his anger at her asking him any kind of question and stopped herself.

"Tell me something. Does your cop know that you carried weight across state lines? Does he know that you brought cocaine from California to Jersey for those idiot cousins of mine?"

"What? I did not! I didn't bring anything but the jacket you said was a family keepsake."

"You didn't know what kind of product was sewn into that jacket. A jacket I got from the Salvation Army, by the way. But, I'm pretty sure your cop won't care.

He's a narc, right? No, he wouldn't understand your moving weight like that."

"But I had no idea. And your cousins weren't selling drugs anymore. They were trying to do the right thing."

"Yeah, they flushed my drugs. Can you believe that?" He shrugged. "So I had to kill them. The only problem is now there's only you left to make up the cash for my product. At first, I was going to let it slide. See, I had other plans for you. Since your brother went to his death trying to keep you from me, because you were supposed to be so pure and perfect. I was all set to court you and keep you in that perfect little bubble world Calvin had you in. But now that you're around here screwing cops, I think I ought to take my money out of your ass. I didn't take the time to have those punk little boyfriends of yours jumped so that you could give it up to a cop.

"I waited a long time for this and I'm not waiting anymore. This is what I've been waiting to taste since you were fifteen. Who would have thought your simple ass would get busted shoplifting and not go through the initiation? Then Calvin made it so none of the others would approach you about joining. Well, he's dead and can't stop me now."

He snatched her up from the ground and started dragging her back out of the room. She dug in her feet and pulled away, flailing her arms and connecting with any part of his body she could. She kicked and punched until he grabbed her and held her still.

She glared at him with all the hatred in her heart. "Did you kill my brother? Did you kill Calvin?"

"Yes, I killed him. And if you keep asking me questions, I will kill you, too." He slapped her and sent her spiraling toward the coffee table. The back of her head hit the end of the table before everything faded to black.

From the moment they saw David Sims enter the house, Lawrence wanted to go right in after him. The guy gave him the creeps and he knew without a doubt he would regret not following his gut.

His superiors, the DEA agent and Detective Morales from the LAPD wanted to get at least a confession out of David.

So they sat there in the garage and listened.

"Why are you here, David?"

Lawrence could hear the attitude in Minerva's voice as she asked the question and he wanted to tell her not to provoke the man. As soon as he thought it he heard the sound of flesh smacking flesh. Steam burst from his head as he made his way to the door, only to be halted by his superior officers from the homicide division.

"He hit her!" Lawrence struggled against the men holding him.

"We need to get the murder confession if we can before we go bursting up in there." Jennings could talk all that sit-and-wait stuff. The woman he loved hadn't just been struck.

Lawrence realized he loved her. "Damn it, I didn't sign on for this and neither did she. I promised her I wasn't going to let anything happen to her."

He was breathing so hard he could barely hear himself

think. But he did hear the ugly tone in Sims's voice. And he heard him hit her again and again. It sounded like she was fighting back and he felt an odd mix of pride and fear. He didn't want her to put herself at risk. But he should have known his little hip-hop feminist warrior goddess of wisdom wouldn't go down without a fight.

He knew that as soon as his colleagues let him go he would probably lose his badge. Excessive force would seem like a pillow fight compared to what he was going to do when he got his hands on David Sims. He gritted his teeth.

"Y'all can let me go."

They kept holding him.

"I'm sorry, David. Please don't hit me again. What did I..."

"Tell me something, does your cop know that you carried weight across state lines? Does he know that you brought cocaine from California to Jersey for those idiot cousin of mine?"

"What? I did not! I didn't bring anything but the jacket you said was a family heirloom."

"You didn't know what kind of product was sewn into the jacket. A jacket I got from the Salvation Army by the way. But, I'm pretty sure your cop won't care. He's a narc, right? No, he wouldn't understand you moving weight like that."

"But I had no idea. And your cousins weren't selling drugs anymore. They were trying to do the right thing."

"Yeah, they flushed my drugs. Can you believe that? So I had to kill them..."

Lawrence wrestled himself from their grip. "I hope y'all have enough, because I'm going in there!"

He burst through the door in the back of the house and made his way as quickly as he could to the front of the house where Minerva and David were. He could tell his colleagues were right behind him. Someone snatched him back before he could get to Sims and they were able to hold him until he saw Minerva on the floor.

"No!" He ran toward her body while they were cuffing Sims. The man's smirk triggered an avalanche of emotions and Lawrence leaped for him. Again his colleagues held him back.

"Come on, Hightower, you don't want to give this asshole any excuses to walk," Detective Morales said, but the man couldn't look Lawrence in the eye.

He could feel his heart breaking as he knelt down beside Minerva. He felt for her pulse and thanked God when he found one. She was bleeding from her nose and her mouth. There was a gash in the back of her head where she had hit the table. And she was out cold.

He had let her down. He had said he would protect her and he let that animal hurt her. He wanted to cradle her in his arms and never let her go, but he was afraid to move her. His heart felt like it was bursting through his chest and a cold fear washed over him. He couldn't lose her.

She had to be okay.

He loved her.

Chapter 16

He needed her to wake up.

The guilt started to close in on him as he sat by her bedside in the stark, cold and sterile hospital room. He willed her to open her eyes. She had drifted in and out of consciousness ever since they brought her in. Luckily, she hadn't needed stitches for the gash in the back of her head. She was a little bruised. But, God willing, she would be okay.

"How is she, son?"

He glanced up and saw his father, James Hightower, in the doorway. He had called the family to let them know what had happened and wasn't surprised to see his father. In fact, he fully expected the entire Hightower clan to show up once word got around. They had all taken a liking to Minerva at the surprise party and they would want to lend their support.

"She's been in and out. I hope she opens her eyes soon." He rubbed his hand across his face in frustration. "Everything just went so wrong, Dad. I failed her. I messed up and she got hurt. I'll never forgive myself for that."

"Let's take a walk, son. Let's go grab a cup of coffee and talk."

Lawrence looked at Minerva. He didn't want to leave her, in case she woke up and was more lucid this time.

"I promise I won't keep you long. Come on. You look like you could use a walk and a strong cup of coffee."

He got up and followed his father but not before taking another glance at his sleeping beauty.

As they stood in line at the hospital café waiting for their coffee, Lawrence's mind stayed on Minerva. He played and replayed everything in his mind. Trying to figure out a way that he could have done better by her. Sure they had gotten David Sims, but at what cost? The woman he loved would never be able to trust him to protect her. She'd gotten hurt under his watch.

"It's not your fault, son."

The hell it wasn't! He should have never allowed her to use herself as bait. "I didn't protect her properly."

"You did the best you could under the circum-stances. You can't beat yourself up about it and let it stop you from the most important part." His father's stern expression gave him pause.

"And what would that be?" he asked as they took their coffee and sat at one of the small green metal café table and chair sets that decorated the place.

"Claiming the woman you love. Letting her know that you intend to do right by her from now on. The way I see it, you are in danger of letting the perfect woman for you get away."

Stunned, he could only look at his father. He had just admitted to himself that he loved Minerva. He hadn't even told her yet and he didn't know if she felt the same way. Hell, he didn't even know if it would last. This was all virgin territory for him.

Instead of admitting his insecurity to the man that he'd been trying to impress since he'd decided to stop being the Hightower screwup and repent for the loss of his cousin's life, Lawrence opted to play it cool.

"I don't know if we're there yet, Dad. We're still getting to know each other. And there was the trust issue. I had to be sure she wasn't a criminal. And now, well, if she stays in town, then I suppose we can explore a relationship. Plus you know, she's got a lot going on, a lot to deal with—"

"Cut the bull, son. This is your father you're talking to. I know you better than you know yourself. And I only have a few things to say on the topic. First, we could all tell at Penny's party the other night that you were a goner. And because we could see how this special young woman had opened you up and put a smile on your face, we became just as smitten with her. You know your mother, she's already dreaming of the wedding and her grand-babies.

"So, you might as well come clean about your feelings so I can properly advise you. What's really holding you back? And it better not be that foolishness you've been spouting over the years about only marrying a woman if she can cook like your mama. Because they don't make 'em like my Celia anymore and you're going to miss out on a great love waiting for that."

Lawrence had to laugh, even if it was a nervous chuckle. How had his father figured out his feelings for Minerva when he was only now starting to figure them out himself?

"Actually, dad, the girl can throw down in the kitchen. She is right up there with Mama. And you're right. I do love her. I just want to make sure she's really the one. For her sake and mine. I'm still getting to know her. She isn't the little 'hood girl hanging with drug dealers I thought she was. She's an amazing college graduate with aspirations to get her master's in social work so that she can help the community. She doesn't just have a smart-aleck mouth. She's actually smart and well read. She's funny. She's sexy as all get-out. And when she looks at me…man… Dad… I just want to be sure. I want to be able to trust what I think I see in her eyes."

"So what is the problem? Are you still worried about proving yourself, based on what happened to Michael? Because at this point in your life, son, you have to know that you're not that same kid. You can't keep living your life trying to make up for something that wasn't your fault."

Lawrence closed his eyes. He thought about what his father said. His feelings for Minerva had nothing to do with the guilt he carried about his cousin.

"At first, I didn't really trust her because of what happened to Michael. I saw what my trusting the wrong person had done and how he basically paid with his life for my misplaced trust. And to tell the truth I haven't even wanted to trust anyone but family since then. And then Minerva came along and…I don't know…I *wanted* to trust her."

"Son, based on everything you've just said, you already have it bad. Let me tell you a little story about a rookie cop whose first beat was down in the Fourth Ward. He was very serious about his job and cleaning up the streets. He strongly upheld his family legacy of honor and didn't want to do anything to call that legacy into question. His parents and his older sister had drummed the mantra of Hightower honor into his head from the time he could understand words. So imagine his reaction when he saw one of the young women from the teen group that his sister mentored out on his streets with a female gang. Not only was she in a gang but she seemed to be the ringleader. And if you think your Minerva had a smart mouth, you should have seen your mother back in the day."

"My mama? Mama was in a gang?" Lawrence couldn't even finish his coffee. His mouth just hung open as he tried to picture his mama in a gang.

"She sure was. They were nothing like these gangs today, but they caused their fair share of trouble. And Celia was as complicated and confusing to figure out as your Minerva. What I later learned was that those girls had been her childhood friends and she kept them from getting into much more trouble than they would have if she weren't with them. And since the Fourth Ward was just as troubled then as it is now, they protected one another. But I couldn't see all of that then. All I could see was she was clearly a liar, a trouble-maker and drop-dead gorgeous to boot."

"I don't believe it. Not my mama…"

"Believe it. And how about your mama used to be really close with your aunt Sophie, too. Sophie was in charge of her sorority's teen program and she had taken a liking to Celia. Sophie saw to it that Celia got the sorority's scholarship for college. And really took her under her wing. She said that the girl had potential and Celia tried her best to live up to the faith that Sophie had in her."

"Okay, now I know you're lying. Aunt Sophie and underprivileged youth? Mentoring Mama? Them being friends? Nah…" Lawrence shook his head in awe and disbelief. He figured there were probably lots of things he didn't know about his parents. But this took the cake.

"I'm telling the truth. They would still be close today and Sophie might not be so troublesome if I hadn't come into the picture."

"Wow…I'm stunned. You would think your falling in love with Mama would have made them closer."

"Maybe if I hadn't done everything in my power to try and prove that Celia was just a gang girl not worthy of the attention Sophie was giving her. I was so bent on proving she was up to no good, I almost threw away the love of my life. By the time Celia was getting ready to graduate from college, I realized that I couldn't fight my feelings anymore. Sophie felt betrayed. She thought that Celia had used their connection to snag a husband. And Celia felt that Sophie had been a fraud who lied because, even though she'd pumped Celia up to believe she could do anything, she didn't think she was good enough for her baby brother or the Hightower name."

Lawrence just stared at his father. He couldn't think of a thing to say.

"But that's their story. The important part of this story is for you. You can learn from my mistakes. I almost lost the woman I loved. There comes a time when you have to trust your own heart. Stop thinking about whether you can trust her, or whether you can trust her feelings for you, or whether she's really trust-worthy, and put some trust and faith in your own heart. What has your heart been telling you from the first time you laid eyes on her? Why did you feel the need to stay so close to her? Do you really think it was just your cop instincts? What is your heart telling you right now? You need to trust someone all right, son. You need to trust *yourself.* Trust your love."

The words his father said felt like a lead weight being lifted off his chest. Why hadn't he seen this before now?

"I gotta go, Dad. Thanks! I love you."

* * *

Minerva woke up to the most intense headache she had ever had. The entire afternoon flashed in her mind and she thanked God she was still alive. She winced as she tried to sit up a little and opted to just lie there instead.

The stark white surroundings, the antiseptic smell and the bars on her bed meant she was in a hospital room. Lawrence wasn't anywhere in sight. So she could only assume that David was right; Lawrence didn't want anything to do with a woman who had carried drugs across state lines.

"So you're awake" a woman's voice came from her right. It had a snide and condescending tone.

When she turned her head to look at the woman, she noticed that the tone matched the facial expression. Her head hurt too much to put up with crap from people she didn't know.

"Who are you and why are you in my room?" Minerva knew she could do snide just as well as the pointy-breasted old lady sporting a tight graying bun on the top of her head.

"My name is Sophie Hightower. I'm the matriarch of the Hightower family. I'm Lawrence's aunt. And I've heard all about you from various family members and my friends here at the hospital. I'm a retired nurse and this was my place of employment for years."

The *Aunt Sophie? The one who all of the Hightower women she'd met at Penny's party had had some kind of run-in with? The one who didn't think any woman but herself was good enough to have the Hightower name? Hmm....*

If the woman's history and condescending tone hadn't already turned Minerva off the self-important I'm-the-queen-of-the-world speech would have done the job just fine. There was really no reason to ask why the woman was there. But she felt like being a smart aleck anyway.

"Okay, now I know who you are. Why are you in my room?"

The woman reared her shoulders back and poked out her ample chest. "I'm here to let you know you are all wrong for my nephew."

"Well, you could have saved your time. I already know that. Anything else?"

Sophie huffed and her back straightened. "If you already know this then why were you shacking up with him all week doing God knows what and dancing with him at that...that *girl's* party."

"You mean Penny's party? It was a wonderful party. I don't remember meeting you there. Were you invited?"

"Please! I wouldn't go to a party for that little street urchin if you paid me. And speaking of street urchins... You have to know that a man like my nephew is too good for you. He needs a woman with class, breeding, not to mention someone closer to his own age. Someone without the stench of drug dealers and gang bangers so close to her..." Sophie tilted her head and turned up her nose as she spoke.

Taller, shapelier, crime-free... Lawrence's words came back to haunt her as she listened to his siddity aunt. As much as the mean old woman was getting on her nerves, she had a point. As much as Minerva loved Lawrence, it wasn't going to work between them. The fact that he wasn't there at that moment spoke volumes.

She blinked back the tears that threatened to fall. She was not going to let Sophie Hightower or the fact that Lawrence didn't want her make her cry. She had gone through too much to let this bring her down.

"Anything else?" She pointedly glared Sophie in the eye, even though her voice cracked under the words. "Because if there's nothing else you feel pressed to let me know, I'd like you to leave now."

"You don't have to be so rude, young lady!"

"*Rude?* Rude is coming into a person's room whom you hardly know and telling her you don't think she is good enough for someone else. Rude is presuming you know enough about a person without saying one word to her, or even having a basic conversation with her, to make any judgments about her worth one way or the other. *You* are rude, Ms. Hightower! But I don't have to suffer your rudeness."

"I am old enough to be your grandmother!"

"And that means I should let you insult me? Please leave or I will call for someone to remove you."

"What's going on in here? Aunt Sophie, what are you doing here?"

Minerva had never been happier to see Lawrence. Even if he didn't want her, at least he could get rid of his annoying aunt. She glanced at him and the concerned expression on his face made her heart melt.

He walked over to her bed and brushed his lips softly across her forehead. The mere touch heated her to the core.

"Sorry I wasn't here when you woke up, baby. I went to grab a cup of coffee with my dad." He narrowed his eyes at his aunt. "I hope Aunt Sophie wasn't bothering you. Why are you in here, Aunt Sophie?"

"I just wanted to meet the young woman. I'll leave since I'm clearly not wanted." Sophie straightened her back and her pointy breasts poked out even farther. "Just remember what I told you, young lady."

"Yeah. Got it. Goodbye." Her voice was snappier than she felt as she pointed toward the door and pursed her lips.

"She's rude, Lawrence, and totally unworthy! I hope you aren't considering getting serious about this one. She's—"

"None of your business or concern, Aunt Sophie. And we'd both like you to leave." Lawrence stepped out of the door and used his arms to signal the way out for Sophie.

"But, Lawrence—"

"Leave. Please," Lawrence barked.

Minerva watched the woman walk out of the room and angrily wiped away a tear that escaped her eye and trickled down her cheek.

The nerve of that tear! I refuse to cry. I'm not going to! She took a deep breath and focused her energy on the sexy cop in her room.

Lawrence wrapped his arms around her. "Seeing you here all bruised and knowing it's my fault is hard. I'm so sorry, baby. I should have protected you better. I'm sorry."

His words and his touch had a soothing effect on her and she was able to calm down a little. But she was still left with the ache in her heart, the ache that came from knowing they weren't going to make it. She wouldn't be able to have him in her life, feel his touch, any of it, for very long.

"I can't believe I almost spazzed out on you again." She pulled away and forced a smile her heart didn't feel.

"You've been through a lot. If anyone deserves to spazz out, it's you. I wish you didn't have to go through any of it. I wish I could have gotten in there before he—"

"If his confession sends him to jail for killing my brother, then it was worth it. I'll heal."

"But will you ever be able to trust me to look out for you, to protect you? I—"

"You have been protecting me all week, whether I wanted you to or not. If it weren't for you, David's goons would have snatched me up and they might have really hurt me in front of the police station. You're my very own Superman. And even he couldn't save Lois Lane all the time. I don't blame you for what happened."

She nibbled her lower lip. "Are they going to arrest me?"

"Arrest you for what?"

"David said that he had me bring drugs to the

McKnight twins in that jacket. I had no idea that anything was sewn in the jacket. I would never have —"

"There's no evidence of that. It would be your word against his with the McKnights dead. No one's going to arrest you. No, the only person going to jail is David Sims. He was charged with selling drugs and the murders, and they are looking into money laundering in relation to some of the small businesses he dealt with as a brokerage agent. He's going away for a long, long time."

"Oh. So I guess I can go back to California when I'm released from here."

He shook his head. "No, you can't."

"Huh? Why not?"

"You said you would stay and we could see where this relationship could go. So you can't go back to California because you're staying here." He brushed his lips across her forehead again and she felt the tingles all the way down to her toes.

It was time for a reality check. Was she the only one of the two of them who realized that things weren't going to work between them? She took a deep breath, as she got ready to do the hardest thing she'd ever done in her life.

Everything inside of him told him to just blurt out that he loved her. And he would have if she didn't have a look on her face like she wanted to bolt out of the room. She was the one. He had to trust his gut no matter what.

"Listen—" he started.

"Lawrence, I—" she started.

They both stopped and the gentleman in him said let the lady go first even though his gut told him he would regret it.

"You go ahead."

"Lawrence, this past week has been amazing. Hell, the past few months with you acting as my personal shadow have been amazing. If I'm honest with myself, I have to admit that I fell for you hard the first time I saw you. And that's why I can't stay. Your aunt, for all her stuck-up opinions, was right. I'm not the right girl for you. You need someone, like she said, 'without the stench of drug dealers and gang bangers.'" She gave a soft smile as tears slid down her cheek. "Maybe someone *taller, shapelier and crime-free.*"

"I want you, Minerva." *Tell her you love her!* The voice inside his head screamed. "You promised you would stay."

"I know. But it would only be putting off the inevitable. My heart is breaking now. But if I stayed and things ended up going to hell later, I don't think I could take it. We could just part friends and…"

Grasping, he threw out the first thing he could think of. "You could be pregnant."

"I know. If I am, I'll be sure to let you know as soon—"

"That's not good enough. I'd like for you to stay here until we know for sure."

She paused and then a hurt expression transformed her face and made him want to kick himself.

Why couldn't he just put his heart on the line and tell her the truth?

"You don't trust me... I... Okay...I'll stay until we know one way or the other, if that's what you want." Her voice cracked. "Can you leave now? I'm tired. I promise I won't escape from the hospital or anything like that. I'm just not in the mood for company right now."

He left feeling like the biggest idiot and the worst kind of jerk combined. He had to find a way to make things right and get the woman he loved to see that they could work.

Chapter 17

Lawrence was going to kill his family. The women in his family were at his home.

"You can just sublet my apartment, Minerva. And it will work out perfectly if you accept the position at Hightower Security that James and Joel offered you. My place is right in Elmwood Park and the offices are right in Fair Lawn. You'll see that you can walk a block in North Jersey and be in another town." Samantha lounged on Lawrence's sofa trying to move Minerva out of his home as if she were discussing the weather or something.

No doubt they meant well. They were trying to be helpful. But in the two weeks since Minerva had been released from the hospital, his family had hovered all around his place with their helpfulness. Lawrence had barely had a chance to tell her how he really felt about her. And now they had figured out a way to talk her into staying in the area. But they were taking her right out of his house.

That wouldn't work at all.

"Of course she'll take the job with Hightower Security. And I'll make sure that James makes her hours really flexible so that she can take classes and get her MSW like she planned. This is going to work out just perfectly." His mother nodded her head in agreement with Samantha.

"I'd be more than happy to take you around to the surrounding colleges and universities to check out the programs," Penny offered.

"But—" Minerva started, clearly overwhelmed.

"If you're going to try and come up with some reason why you have to go back to California, just forget it. You're family now. We've claimed you. And I couldn't bear the thought of one of mine out there on her own," Celia interrupted as she patted Minerva's arm and looked at Penny and Samantha for backup.

"What if she doesn't want to move? What if she wants to stay here with me?" Lawrence had to interject. If he let his mother, Samantha and Penny go on, they would have her moved out by the end of the day.

All four women turned and glared at him before turning back and continuing with their conversation as if he hadn't even spoken, even his own Mama. This was getting out of hand.

"Minerva…" he started, but realized he didn't want the Hightower wives and fiancée brigade around when he tried yet again to talk to the woman he loved and more than likely experience her rebuff.

All four women turned and cut him disparaging looks. This time they stared at him as if they were all waiting to see what he would deign to say.

"Never mind, we can talk once your new posse leaves," he muttered ruefully.

"She's going with us. We're going to spend the day at the spa and then tonight it's Samantha's bachelorette party. You guys have the bachelor party tonight," Penny offered with a smirk.

He'd forgotten about all the wedding hoopla. Joel and Samantha's wedding was only a week away.

"And you have to come to the wedding, too, Minerva. I don't want to hear any excuses. You can even bring a date. I could maybe hook you up with someone." Samantha turned and cast her mischievous eyes on him.

"There's this really nice young man at church." His mother patted her chin with her pointer finger as if in concentration.

"Hey! Mama! She doesn't need a date. Minerva, can I please talk to you for a minute? And before you all turn and glare at me like I'm the spawn of Satan, just save it. Minerva. A minute. Please."

She stood and followed him to his study. She looked so beautiful he just wanted to pull her into his arms and kiss her until she agreed to stay with him forever. And he did want forever in her arms.

"What do you want?" she asked with a sigh.

"You." He knew he had to sound earnest because he had never felt this much need in all his life. He wanted her and he needed her to believe that.

"I'm here. What do you want with me? What do you have to say to me?"

"I want you, Minerva. *I want you.* The last two weeks have been hell. You're here and you're barely talking to me. And now my entire family has decided to champion your cause and they're all against me, even my own mama!"

"Hey! I didn't turn them against you." She took a step back shaking her head.

He couldn't go much longer without touching her. Two weeks was long enough. He pulled her into his arms.

She pulled away from him, only giving him a moment of connection.

"This is not a good idea. I'm not doing this dance with you anymore, Lawrence. We're from two totally different worlds. So this whole 'I want you' thing is pointless. It can't go anywhere."

"That's not true. Look, here's the thing. I love you, baby. *I love you.* And I want you. I want you here with me."

Her eyes widened and she took two steps backward before turning and leaving the room.

Deciding not to go after her, and instead to give her time to process what he had just confessed, was the hardest decision he had ever made. He just hoped it was the right one.

* * *

After a night of wild talk and games with the women in Lawrence's family, Minerva was beat. Those women knew how to have a great time and they knew how to get knee-deep in folks' business. Between Celia's proclamations that Lawrence and Minerva's wedding would be next, and Carla's claiming Minerva as her newly adopted second child, Minerva had gotten more than enough advice.

"You're back."

Lawrence sat on the sofa and his deep masculine voice greeted her as soon as she walked in the door. She wished his voice didn't have such an impact on her, but it did.

"Hey, you're back early yourself. I thought for sure the wild bachelor party would still be going on."

"Nope, you ladies out-partied us. I've been home for over an hour." He smiled at her and she had to catch her breath.

"Oh. You didn't have to wait up."

"Yes, I did. I need to talk to you, baby."

She took a deep breath and sat down next to him on the sofa. She kept her eyes pinned on her feet and hands, anywhere but on him. Out of all the advice she'd gotten from the women, the majority of that advice told her to believe Lawrence when he said he loved her. And she wanted to. God, did she want to.

"I love you."

Her pulse began to race.

"No, you don't. How could you when you don't

trust me? You don't even trust me to go back to California before we find out if I'm pregnant. You don't trust me to be up front with you about something like that. So what if I am pregnant? Do you trust me to be the mother of your child?" They were from opposite sides of the tracks. She hadn't really realized how hurt she was by that until she heard her voice. She felt her own pain through each crack and catch.

"I *want* you to be the mother of my children. Baby, I love you. I didn't want you to leave and go back to California. So I grasped at the first idiotic thing to come to my mind. I trust you with all my heart. Girl, you *are* my heart. And I just want a chance to make you fall in love with me as much as I am with you. I want you to stay."

She inhaled and exhaled in quick succession.

Believe him.

He reached out and caressed her cheek, turning her to face him. "I've never experienced fear like what I felt when I couldn't reach you in time to stop David Sims from hurting you. And the guilt… I know I'll carry it for the rest of my life. But I'm not going to let guilt and my troubles with trusting my feelings keep me from love. I kept thinking, after my cousin died, that I didn't deserve to be happy. And all I focused on was proving I wasn't a screwup and doing the right thing.

"I didn't trust myself to feel anything for anyone but my family and a few close friends. I never let a woman get close enough to penetrate my barriers. And then I saw you… And from the first moment I saw you, even with that crazy two-toned hair, you pushed against and past all my walls. You had me loving you in spite of all the feelings I'd worked so hard to resist and everything I thought I knew about you. Baby, I couldn't have been more wrong, and I can't be more sorry. I just hope you are willing to give me a chance to show you how much I love you."

His eyes sucked her right in.

"Lawrence, you are the most amazing man I've ever known. You say I pushed past your barriers. But I say you drew me to you. I couldn't resist you, even though you worked my last nerves from the first moment. I am so in love with you. And I have wanted to tell you that from the first moment your lips touched mine. But I'm so scared. I don't think I could take it if you decided you didn't want me anymore. It's my whole heart on the line, my entire being. And I still feel like it might not be enough. We come from such different worlds, such different backgrounds."

As she spoke, she made peace with her decision. He shook his head and pulled her closer to him. "If you love me half as much as I love you, then none of that matters. Do you really love me, baby?"

The strength of his embrace made her feel safe and secure. She loved him even more. "Yes. I do. And I'll stay in Jersey so that we can give our relationship a chance. But I think it would be best if I sublet Samantha's apartment and took the job at Hightower Security. I know you offered to let me stay here and help me with paying for my MSW. But I don't want to be a kept woman. I can pay my own way."

He frowned. "But I want you here with me. I see forever in your eyes, baby. We will make it last. This is the real thing."

"I believe that." As she said it, she realized she really did mean it. "But I still think we should have our own space while we continue to get to know one another. I'm serious about not wanting to be a kept woman, Lawrence. This is important to me. Your aunt already thinks I'm not good enough for you. Just imagine what she'll have to say if I moved in and let you take care of me."

"Aunt Sophie has issues." Lawrence waved his hand in annoyance. "And you *won't* be a kept woman."

"I know I won't because I'm not going to allow myself to become one." She knew she was making the right decision. They were going to make it work, the right way.

He just smiled at her. "We'll talk about this later. Right now, I just want you to say you love me again."

"And I want you to say you love me again and again and again," she teased.

"I love you, Minerva."

"I love you, Lawrence."

Epilogue

"You may now kiss your bride."

Lawrence's brother, Joel, didn't seem like he had to be told twice. His head was already bent and he was swooping in before the minister finished the word *bride*.

Minerva turned her gaze away from the smooching couple and took note of her handsome man, standing there at his brother's side, looking as good as he wanted to look in his tuxedo. He certainly was the best man, even if she was just a *tad* bit biased.

He winked as he smiled at her and she winked back as the goose bumps popped all over her body and the butterflies danced and fluttered in her belly.

She didn't know if it was the beautifully decorated

church, all done up in rustic flowers that belied the ending of fall, or the beautiful rust gowns that the bridesmaids wore, but she could feel love all around her. And after the death and loss that had haunted her the past few months, it felt good.

The flowing cream gown Samantha wore looked like something right out of a fairy tale. The color contrast between the gown and her smooth chocolate skin was breathtaking. The strapless dress had intricate beadwork on its bodice and layers and layers of raw silk on the skirt. Her jet-black natural hair was swept up in a sparkling tiara. She looked gorgeous, and Minerva couldn't help wondering if she would look half as pretty on her own wedding day.

The wedding reception was held in a posh hotel ballroom and the entire décor epitomized elegance. The same rustic floral arrangements from the church graced the ballroom and the color scheme of rust and the most majestic-looking purple she'd ever seen took shape in layers of silk and crepe. It looked like royalty was getting married and it was a sight to behold.

Dressed in her own stunning red backless gown, Minerva felt like royalty herself as Lawrence swept her around the dance floor. The bride and groom had shared their special dance and the dance floor was now crowded with guests. No matter how many people surrounded them, she couldn't take her eyes off Lawrence.

"You look beautiful." He bent down and brushed her lips with his. "I love you."

"I love you, too. More than you'll ever know." She

couldn't believe just how easy it was to express how she felt about this man. She didn't think she would ever get tired of telling him she loved him.

They danced just about every dance together. Close. Connected. One. Neither of them wanted to part when it came time for the single men and women to do the age-old garter and bouquet catch. But no one in the family would let them sit it out.

Minerva stood in the circle of women not really trying to catch anything. She smiled when Samantha looked back and winked at her before tossing the beautiful flowers. They landed right in her arms and she clutched them tight to her chest just in time to stop this really mean-looking sister from snatching them away.

She watched as they literally dragged all the single men onto the floor and noticed that Lawrence's older brother Patrick was oddly missing.

None of the men seemed to be focused on Joel. In fact, they seemed to be doing their best not to pay attention to Joel or where he aimed the frilly blue lace garter. The only one who looked like he was waiting to catch the thing was Lawrence. And catch it he did.

Before she knew it, she was being swept onto the middle of the floor and plopped unto a chair. She held her breath as Lawrence slipped the garter belt up her thigh in an achingly slow manner. The "coincidence" of her catching Samantha's bridal bouquet and Lawrence catching the garter belt no longer took center stage in her mind. She wasn't even thinking about the crowd of people standing around them in the posh ballroom.

They might have been the center of attention at the moment. But all she could think about was Lawrence's hand caressing her thigh as he put the garter in place.

She stared at him as he kneeled on one knee in front of her. He gazed up at her with an intensity that made her breath catch in her throat and her heart thud with the force of a thunderstorm. She opened her mouth and closed it.

"Are you done?" Her question came out in a soft panting whisper.

He shook his head before responding. "No." He reached for her hand and led her away from the dance floor. They walked in silence out onto the balcony.

He bent down and covered her mouth with his. The kiss was the perfect mix of gentle and all-consuming. The teasing nibbles of his teeth and flicks of his tongue turned her inside out and back again.

She gulped and traced his loving mouth as if she were trying to commit the shape and frame to sensory memory.

"I could kiss you all day." He caressed the side of her face and trailed down to the base of her neck as he stopped the kiss and pulled away.

She smiled because he hadn't said anything she didn't feel ten times over.

He reached into his pocket and pulled out a ring box. "I've been waiting for the right time to do this. And now seems like the perfect time."

"Lawrence?" This couldn't be what she thought it was. Could it? He couldn't be asking her to marry him.

She wasn't pregnant. They had gotten proof of that

the morning after they confessed their love for each other. If he was asking her to marry him, it wasn't because he felt obligated. He must really want to.

"I love you with all my heart and soul, Minerva Jones. I want to spend the rest of my life with you. I want to be there beside you when you accomplish all the amazing goals you have for your life. I want you to be the mother of my children. I want you to stay with me, forever. Loving you has made me a better man than I ever could have dreamed of being. I trust you with my life, with my heart. I said you wouldn't be a kept woman because I already knew that you would be my wife. Please help me to be an honest man and say you'll be my wife. Will you marry me, Minerva?"

He opened the box and the most beautiful ring she'd ever seen glimmered inside. The emerald-cut diamond sparkled so brightly it sent rays of sunlight through its prisms.

He loved her and he wanted to marry her. Her heart felt so full it threatened to burst wide open.

"I love you, Lawrence. And I can't think of anything I'd rather do than be your wife. Yes. I'll marry you. You sure about this, Detective? I plan on making this a life sentence for you with no possibility for parole. You'll be stuck with me." She gazed lovingly in his eyes.

"That's exactly what I was hoping for. Anything else would be criminal. Punishable to the full extent of the law, baby."

"Really, the law, huh? Well since I'm living crime-free these days, I wouldn't want to do anything to get me in trouble with the law. What law would I be breaking by the way?"

He grinned before standing and swooping her up. "The law of desire, baby." Then he covered her lips in a searing kiss.

Should she believe the facts?

Essence bestselling author

DONNA HILL

SEDUCTION AND LIES

Book 2 of the TLC miniseries

Hawking body products for Tender Loving Care is just a
cover. The real deal? They're undercover operatives for a
covert organization. Newest member Danielle Holloway's first
assignment is to infiltrate an identity-theft ring. But when the
clues lead to her charismatic beau, Nick Mateo, Danielle has
more problems than she thought.

TLC —There's more to these ladies than Tender Loving Care!

Coming the first week of December wherever books are sold.

KIMANI
ROMANCE™

www.kimanipress.com

KPDH0921208

They had nothing in common—
except red-hot desire!

National bestselling author

Marcia King-Gamble

TEMPTING
MOGUL
the

Life coach Kennedy Fitzgerald's assignment
grooming unconventional, sexy Salim Washington
to take over as TV studio head has become a little
too pleasurable. For both of them. But shady
motivations and drama threaten to stall this
merger before the ink's even dry!

Coming the first week of December
wherever books are sold.

KIMANI™
ROMANCE

www.kimanipress.com KPMKG0931208

Will she let her past decide her future?

NATIONAL BESTSELLING AUTHOR
Melanie Schuster

trust
IN
Me

Playboy Lucien Deveraux is ready to settle
down and be a one-woman man. Trouble is,
Nicole Argonne has no time for "pretty boys"—
especially the reformed-player type. If Lucien
wants her, he needs to prove himself...and
Nicole's not going to make it easy.

"A richly satisfying love story."
—*Romantic Times BOOKreviews* on *Let It Be Me*

*Coming the first week of December
wherever books are sold.*

KIMANI™
ROMANCE

www.kimanipress.com

KPMS0951208

REQUEST YOUR FREE BOOKS!

2 FREE NOVELS
PLUS 2 FREE GIFTS!

KIMANI ™
ROMANCE

Love's ultimate destination!

YES! Please send me 2 FREE Kimani™ Romance novels and my 2 FREE gifts (gifts are worth about $10). After receiving them, if I don't wish to receive any more books, I can return the shipping statement marked "cancel." If I don't cancel, I will receive 4 brand-new novels every month and be billed just $4.69 per book in the U.S. or $5.24 per book in Canada, plus 25¢ shipping and handling per book and applicable taxes, if any*. That's a savings of over 20% off the cover price! I understand that accepting the 2 free books and gifts places me under no obligation to buy anything. I can always return a shipment and cancel at any time. Even if I never buy another book from Kimani Press, the two free books and gifts are mine to keep forever.

168 XDN EF2D   368 XDN EF3T

Name	(PLEASE PRINT)	
Address		Apt. #
City	State/Prov.	Zip/Postal Code

Signature (if under 18, a parent or guardian must sign)

Mail to **The Reader Service:**
IN U.S.A.: P.O. Box 1867, Buffalo, NY 14240-1867
IN CANADA: P.O. Box 609, Fort Erie, Ontario L2A 5X3

Not valid to current subscribers of Kimani Romance books.

Want to try two free books from another line?
Call 1-800-873-8635 or visit www.morefreebooks.com.

* Terms and prices subject to change without notice. N.Y. residents add applicable sales tax. Canadian residents will be charged applicable provincial taxes and GST. Offer not valid in Quebec. This offer is limited to one order per household. All orders subject to approval. Credit or debit balances in a customer's account(s) may be offset by any other outstanding balance owed by or to the customer. Please allow 4 to 6 weeks for delivery. Offer available while quantities last.

Your Privacy: Kimani Press is committed to protecting your privacy. Our Privacy Policy is available online at www.eHarlequin.com or upon request from the Reader Service. From time to time we make our lists of customers available to reputable third parties who may have a product or service of interest to you. If you would prefer we not share your name and address, please check here. ☐

KROM08R

One moment can change your life....

Seduced BY Moonlight

NATIONAL BESTSELLING AUTHOR

Janice Sims

When Harrison Payne sees an intriguing stranger
basking in the night air at his Colorado resort,
he's determined to get to know her much better.
Discovering that Cherisse Washington is the
mother of a promising young skier he's agreed
to sponsor is a stroke of luck; learning Cherisse's
ex is determined to get her back is an unwanted
setback. But all's fair in love and war....

*Coming the first wefi of December
wherever books are sold.*

ARABESQUE®

www.kimanipress.com

KPJS1121208

Love, honor and cherish...

•

i promise

NATIONAL BESTSELLING AUTHOR

ADRIANNE byrd

Beautiful, brilliant Christian McKinley could set the world afire. Instead, she dreams of returning to her family's Texas ranch. But Malcolm Williams has other plans for her, publicly proposing to Christian at the social event of the year. So how can she tactfully turn down a proposal from this gorgeous, well-connected, obscenely rich suitor? By inadvertently falling in love with his twin brother, Jordan!

"Byrd proves once again that she's a wonderful storyteller."—*Romantic Times BOOKreviews* on *The Beautiful Ones*

Coming the first wefi of December wherever books are sold.

ARABESQUE®

www.kimanipress.com   KPAB1151208

Their marriages were shams,
but their payback will be real....

Counterfeit
Wives

Fan-favorite author
PHILLIP THOMAS DUCK

Todd Darling was the perfect husband…to three
women. Seduced and betrayed, Nikki, Jacqueline
and Dawn learned too late their dream marriage
was an illusion. Struggling to rebuild their lives,
they're each invited by a mysterious woman to
learn more about the husband they thought they
knew. But on a journey filled with surprises, the
greatest revelations will be the truths they learn
about themselves....

Coming the first week of December
wherever books are sold.

sepia™

www.kimanipress.com KPPTD1291208

NATIONAL BESTSELLING AUTHOR

ROCHELLE ALERS

invites you to meet the Whitfields of New York....

Tessa, Faith and Simone Whitfield know all about coordinating
other people's weddings, and not so much about arranging
their own love lives. But in the space of one unforgettable year,
all three will meet intriguing men who just might bring them their
very own happily ever after....

Long Time Coming

June 2008

The Sweetest Temptation

July 2008

Taken by Storm

August 2008

ARABESQUE®

www.kimanipress.com

KPALERSTRIL08